The Golden Imaginarium

HITHER & NIGH

The Golden Imaginarium

ELLEN POTTER

MARGARET K. MCELDERRY BOOKS

NEW YORK   LONDON   TORONTO   SYDNEY   NEW DELHI

MARGARET K. McELDERRY BOOKS
An imprint of Simon & Schuster Children's Publishing Division
1230 Avenue of the Americas, New York, New York 10020

This book is a work of fiction. Any references to historical events, real people, or real places are used fictitiously. Other names, characters, places, and events are products of the author's imagination, and any resemblance to actual events or places or persons, living or dead, is entirely coincidental.

Text © 2023 by Ellen Potter
Cover illustration © 2023 by Jennifer Bricking
Cover design by Karyn Lee

MARGARET K. McELDERRY BOOKS is a trademark of Simon & Schuster, LLC.
Simon & Schuster: Celebrating 100 Years of Publishing in 2024
For information about special discounts for bulk purchases, please contact Simon & Schuster Special Sales at 1-866-506-1949 or business@simonandschuster.com.
The Simon & Schuster Speakers Bureau can bring authors to your live event. For more information or to book an event, contact the Simon & Schuster Speakers Bureau at 1-866-248-3049 or visit our website at www.simonspeakers.com.
Also available in a Margaret K. McElderry Books hardcover edition
Interior design by Irene Metaxatos
The text for this book was set in Joanna Nova.
Manufactured in the United States of America
0824 BID
First Margaret K. McElderry Books paperback edition October 2024
10 9 8 7 6 5 4 3 2 1
The Library of Congress has cataloged the hardcover edition as follows:
Names: Potter, Ellen, 1963– author. | Potter, Ellen, 1963– Hither & Nigh.
Title: The golden imaginarium / Ellen Potter.
Description: First edition. | New York : Margaret K. McElderry Books, [2023] | Series: Hither & Nigh 2 | Audience: Ages 8 to 12. | Audience: Grades 4–6. | Summary: Weeks after discovering the Nigh and leaving her brother behind, Nell and her friends are given the opportunity to become Watchers, but they must pass three challenging trials with their Nigh creatures called Fates, while also evading the Minister and her Magicians.
Identifiers: LCCN 2023010731 (print) | LCCN 2023010732 (ebook) | ISBN 9781665910422 (hardcover) | ISBN 9781665910439 (paperback) | ISBN 9781665910446 (ebook)
Subjects: CYAC: Magic—Fiction. | Imaginary creatures—Fiction. | Friendship—Fiction. | New York (N. Y.)—Fiction. | Fantasy. | LCGFT: Fantasy fiction. | Novels.
Classification: LCC PZ7.P8518 Gq 2023 (print) | LCC PZ7.P8518 (ebook) | DDC [Fic]—dc23
LC record available at https://lccn.loc.gov/2023010731
LC ebook record available at https://lccn.loc.gov/2023010732

For Marieanne

1

MR. BOOT'S URGENT MESSAGE

When you are massively unpopular in school, you will usually wind up with a lab partner who is certifiably bananas. I present to you exhibit A: Gretchen Mousekey. After our biology teacher, Mrs. Grummund, told us to buddy up, the whole class went into this frenzied game of musical lab partners. Gretchen Mousekey and I were the last ones standing.

"Can you . . . just. . . . Can you *stop* that?" I whispered to Gretchen as she cleaned out her ear with one of the toothpicks we were supposed to use for the experiment.

"Why does it bother you?" Gretchen asked. She was sitting so close to me I could hear the toothpick scraping around in her ear canal. That's the other thing about Gretchen—she has no concept of personal space.

"Why? Because number one, it's totally disgusting," I said, "and number two, you're going to shish kebab your brain."

Mrs. Grummund had been explaining how to put methylene blue on a microscope slide to look at cells from our cheeks, but now she stopped cold. She clasped her hands in front of her and stared at me. I shut up right away.

All the other kids turned to look at me too, a bunch of them with smirks on their faces. I was public enemy number one after causing Tom, an eighth grader whom half the school was crushing on, to be expelled. Except it wasn't my fault, not strictly speaking. And Tom wasn't strictly a boy, not a human one anyway.

"Since you don't appear to need my instructions, Nell," said Mrs. Grummund, "you can demonstrate to the class how to examine squamous epithelial cells under a microscope."

I knew she expected me to cave and grovel. I probably should have, but I was in a strange mood that day. I'd seen something that morning that made me feel all squirrelly inside. And when I feel squirrelly, I get mad. And when I get mad, I do stupid things.

"No problem," I told her.

I snatched up one of the toothpicks from the cup. While the whole class watched, I scraped the inside of my cheek with the toothpick. It felt like putting deodorant on in public. I wiped the toothpick on my microscope slide, topped it off with a few drops of methylene blue, plopped a cover slip on it, and placed it under the microscope. Boom.

"She's done this before, Mrs. Grummund," Leilani objected. She was a tall, square-jawed girl who harbored a special brand of hatred for me. Thankfully, she wasn't in

Mr. Boot's after-school club, because if that girl knew even a speck of magic, she'd be lobbing curses at me like tennis balls at a border collie. "Nell's been kicked out of, like, three other schools."

"Four," I muttered under my breath.

"She said four schools," Gretchen corrected Leilani loudly as she worked a toothpick around the outer edges of her ear. "She was kicked out of four other schools."

There was some giggling in the class, but Leilani was shooting eye bullets at me.

Mrs. Grummund clapped three times. That was supposed to settle everybody down, which you wouldn't think would actually work with a group of seventh graders, except that it almost always did.

"Nell, please look in the microscope and tell the class what you see," said Mrs. Grummund.

I pressed my eye to the microscope lens. Several blue-stained globules began to move around. They stretched and thinned and curled, forming spidery words:

THIS IS AN URGENT MESSAGE FROM MR. BOOT.

A few weeks ago, I would have been totally shocked to see those words appear on the microscope slide. But that was before I joined the Last Chance Club, where weird stuff happened on a fairly regular basis.

"Can I look?" Gretchen was standing right behind me, so close that I could smell her Cheerios breath.

"No." I kept my eye pressed against the microscope so that she wouldn't nudge her way in.

"Nell, please describe what you see," Mrs. Grummund said.

"Um." I tried to remember what a regular epithelial cell had looked like. "There's some blobby stuff?"

There was an eruption of giggles in the class.

"A good scientist is specific, Nell," said Mrs. Grummund. "'Blobby' is not specific."

A loud snort came from Leilani's direction.

I looked back down at the microscope. The previous message was gone and there was a new one in its place:

THERE WILL BE A GUEST AT THE LAST CHANCE CLUB TODAY. THE GUEST IS NOT A HUMAN. DO NOT STARE. DO NOT MAKE THE GUEST MAD. DO WATCH YOUR MOUTH. (AND BY YOUR MOUTH, MR. BOOT MEANS ME. YOUR SQUAMOUS EPITHELIAL CELLS. GET IT? LOL.)

A nonhuman guest? Well, that was a wide playing field. A nonhuman guest could be just about anything—a Sylph or a Fainting Faun. I wouldn't have minded seeing one of those. But knowing Mr. Boot it was probably something a whole lot less pleasant. Something with serrated teeth and eyeballs that squirted poison. Plus, not making someone mad was going to be a stretch for the Last Chance Club, since Crud,

Annika, and I were basically pros at getting ourselves into trouble.

"Nell?"

I looked up. Mrs. Grummund and the whole entire class were staring at me.

"Sorry." I put my eye back on the microscope, trying to remember what cheek cells looked like *specifically*. "They are . . . they're sort of . . ."

The cells were reforming into another message now.

"Let me have a look." Gretchen draped herself against me like a human backpack, pressing her head against mine so that she could maneuver her way to the eyepiece. I stepped on her foot and she quickly backed off.

The new message said:

AND BY THE WAY, THE INSIDE OF YOUR
MOUTH SMELLS LIKE A DUMPSTER

Well, I had hummus on a bagel for breakfast, so what do you expect?

Someone in the class screamed, and when I looked up, everyone was staring at me in horror.

My first thought was that I must have said the thing about the hummus out loud. I spend a lot of time alone. I've definitely been known to talk to myself. But then I noticed they weren't staring at me exactly but at something just behind me.

Gretchen.

More specifically—since Mrs. Grummund wanted specifics—they were staring at Gretchen's right ear, which was bleeding like a stuck pig.

"What's everyone looking at?" Gretchen asked, holding up the bloody toothpick, baffled as to why she was suddenly the center of attention.

"Congratulations, you've poked a hole in your ear," I told her.

The sudden appearance of blood outside the body can really show you what people are made of. John Shultz, a six-foot-tall basketball star and school legend, puked; Mrs. Grummund just stood there with her hand clamped over her mouth. No one seemed to know what to do. But then I remembered the time when a hair stylist had accidentally nicked my ear with a scissor, making it bleed like mad. "Don't worry, honey, it's nothing," she had told me. "The ears are the drama queens of the body."

So I sucked it up and examined Gretchen's ear. It was pretty gory. Her ear was filled with blood and it was overflowing and snaking down her jaw onto her clothes. I ran over to the sink, grabbed a few paper towels, and sopped up the blood. That hair stylist might not have been great at cutting hair, but she was 100 percent right about ears. After I mopped all the blood away, I saw that it came from the tiniest scrape.

Since I now appeared to be Gretchen's self-appointed caregiver, Mrs. Grummund had me escort Gretchen to the nurse's office. Before we left, I managed to pull the slide out from under the microscope and shove it into my back pocket.

At least I wouldn't have to answer any more questions about epithelial cells. Now the only thing I had to worry about, besides Gretchen threatening to ask Mrs. Grummund if we could be permanent lab partners, was whether Mr. Boot's "special guest" was a Moss Neck or a Boggedy Cat or some other terrifying creature, and what it would do to us if we ticked it off. Which, if history was any guide, we probably would.

2

The Leftovers Table

I was dying to talk to Annika and Crud about Mr. Boot's message, but they were both in the eighth grade and I was in the seventh. That meant I had to wait until lunchtime to check in with them. And even then it would be tricky.

At lunch I took my usual seat at the Leftovers Table. It's called the Leftovers Table because it's where all the kids who don't fit in at the other tables sit. We're the friend-group refugees, our own little tribe of free-range weirdos.

Annika was sitting at the Goddess Table. That's where the school's beautiful people sit. While the rest of us are shoveling food in our face holes, the girls at the Goddess Table—with a carefully curated boy or two tossed in—laugh and whisper and play with each other's hair. It looks like a slumber party has spontaneously erupted in the middle of a prison cafeteria.

Annika was sitting at the end of the table, laughing with the rest of them. With her fine-boned features and polished curtain of mahogany hair, Annika was easily the most beautiful of all the goddesses—something I don't love to admit since she and I have a long and difficult history. It was only recently that we had called a truce, and had maybe even grown slightly fond of each other. Yes, it had taken a few scrapes with death to get us there, but never mind. To be honest, it irked me that Annika was still sitting at the Goddess Table after everything we'd been through together in the last few weeks. I had thought she'd join me at the Leftovers Table, like Crud had. We'd all become a team, really. But I guess Annika was too worried about what her glitterati friends would say if she started eating lunch with me, aka school pariah, and Crud, a supersized thug. Not to mention Ruth.

I glanced over at the table in the far corner—the Elsewhere Table, where the foreign exchange students sat.

The table where Tom used to sit.

Tom, the Imp.

It was stupid, I know, but there was a little part of me that half expected he'd just suddenly appear there again one day, wearing that dumb Viking hat, eating Twizzlers and grinning at me.

I glanced to the left and locked eyes with Leilani at the Goddess Table. She had caught me staring at Tom's old spot. She lowered her eyelids to half-mast and shook her head in disgust. Then she leaned over to the girl next to her and whispered something. The girl's eyes flickered toward me, her face squinching up with distaste.

"Hey, kid."

I swiveled around to see Ruth plop down in the seat across from me. She was tall and gangly, with a shoulder-length pageboy, cut so sharply you could slice an apple on it.

"No word from him yet?" She pulled out a sub from a bag marked *Rocco's*, the restaurant that her family owned.

"No word from who?" I asked.

Ruth tipped her head toward the Elsewhere Table, meowed, and then winked at me.

"I'm assuming you mean Tom?" I tried to keep my voice dignified.

"You assume correctly, my good woman."

"Tom moved to Florida," I lied.

I'm not proud of it, but I'm a decent liar. It comes from all those years of playing with the chess hustlers in Washington Square Park. They taught me how to read people's body language at the chess tables. It's important to pick up on those cues because, if you don't, it can cost you a game. They taught me to notice if a player moves their pawn timidly or if they slide it across the board like a hero. If a player seems impatient, they might rush in to capture your queen without seeing the trap you laid for them. Playing with those hustlers was a master class in deceit.

"I'm really sorry, kid." Ruth did sound sorry too, which embarrassed me. I didn't love having her know how much I missed Tom. I shrugged and bit into my mozzarella and tomato sandwich.

A moment later Crud lumbered over to us, carrying a tray of school-lunch meatballs and spaghetti. Everyone on his side of the table shifted over to make room for his bulk, and also because they were a little afraid of him. He had a dangerous reputation in our school. Rumor was that he ate kittens (totally untrue) and that he tried to strangle one of his teachers (true, but there were extenuating circumstances).

"Hey," he grunted at us.

Ruth stared down at his lunch pointedly.

"What?" Crud asked her.

"Yeah . . . so this garbage?" Ruth pointed at Crud's tray of meatballs. "That's not your lunch."

She shoved Crud's tray away from him with her index finger, as if it were a dead squirrel. Reaching into her Rocco's bag, she pulled out a covered plastic dish, and placed it in front of him.

"This is your lunch."

I shot Ruth a grateful smile. The girl was a good egg. Although Crud never said as much, I was pretty sure his family didn't have a lot of money. For one thing, not many kids ate school lunch, and he wolfed that slop down. And for another, I know that he went to the library to do his homework, which probably meant he didn't have a computer at home.

"Thanks," Crud muttered with some embarrassment as he took the container of food and pulled back the lid. Inside was a hefty serving of chicken parmesan, with fat slices of Italian bread on the side. I saw his eyebrows twitch with pleasure.

"I'll find a good home for this." Ruth grabbed his tray and headed toward the trash can at the other end of the lunchroom.

"So," Crud said to me quietly, "did you get a strange message today?"

"Yep. In Biology lab. Under the microscope." We had to be very careful about what we said in public. We were still under Mr. Boot's Gaggen-Shtoppin Spell, which meant we couldn't speak openly about the club. If anyone overheard us, something unpleasant would invariably happen to shut us up. As in, a bunch of ceiling tiles might magically crash down on our skulls. Mr. Boot's Gaggen-Shtoppin Spell took no prisoners.

"Any idea what it means?" Crud asked.

"Not a clue."

He narrowed his eyes at me but said nothing.

"What?"

"You're acting weird," he said. "And not just because of the . . . you know, message. You're acting weird weird."

I hadn't known Crud for very long, but in that short time we'd been through a lot together. It's hard to hide stuff from someone when you have that kind of history with them.

"All right." I sighed. I reached into my backpack, pulled out a bit of torn paper, and handed it to him. "I found it this morning. That's why I'm acting weird weird."

3

THE NOTE

On the door to my apartment building was a faded poster with a photo of my brother River. Above the photo were the words STILL MISSING. It never failed to make my heart pinch every time I saw his ten-year-old face looking back at me. His dark eyes seem poised on a question, as though he knew his life was about to take a strange turn.

And it did. One bright sunny morning, my brother vanished from Washington Square Park. For three years my dad and I searched for him. For three years we lived in hope that he was still alive, somewhere, but with each passing year that seemed more and more impossible. Then I joined the Last Chance Club, and impossible things, *magical things*, began to happen all the time. Suddenly the world was not what I'd thought it was. In fact, I had discovered that there were two worlds: our world, which was called the Hither, and another world that was hidden from us but just a hairsbreadth away, if you knew how to find it. That world was called the Nigh, and it was where River was, trapped, until I could find a way to get him home safely.

Crud read what was written on the scrap of paper I had handed him. "I don't get it. What is this?"

"Someone wrote that in the corner of River's poster."

Scrawled across it, as if it were written in a hurry, was a note:

THERE MAY BE A WAY TO BRING HIM HOME.
THE GOLDEN IMAGINARIUM.

"What's the golden imaginarium?" Crud asked.

"I have no idea."

"It sounds like a video game." Crud turned to the kid across from us—a hard-core gamer. "Hey."

The boy looked up from his lunch. His eyes widened when he saw who was talking to him.

"What's the golden imaginarium?" Crud asked the kid.

"I, uh . . . what? A golden imaginarium? I, um . . ." He looked genuinely terrified, as though Crud was going to throttle him if he didn't give him the right answer. "I've never heard of it. I'm sorry."

Crud handed the note back to me. "I don't know, Nell. I mean, it could just be someone messing with you."

"Who would do that though?"

Crud raised an eyebrow, then jerked his chin toward the Goddess Table. "Take your pick."

I sighed. He might be right. Any one of those girls,

with the exception of Annika, might be vindictive enough to write that note. Still, the wording of the note seemed too on the nose. It didn't say YOU CAN FIND HIM. It said THERE MAY BE A WAY TO BRING HIM HOME.

"Oh, I almost forgot to tell you guys." Ruth plopped down in her seat and slapped her hands on the table. "It's Spooktober week at the Barton Theater. *Carnival of Souls* is playing tonight. Who's in?"

"I'd be up for that," Crud said immediately.

I suspected Crud would be up for anything that Ruth suggested. Mani-pedis, parasailing. Anything.

"What about you, kid?" Ruth asked me.

"Nope. I hate horror movies."

Which was true. But also, this thing sounded a lot like a date.

"Come on, Nell," Crud said. "You should go."

There was something in the way he looked at me, with his brows pinched tensely, that made me think he was not just being polite. In fact, it seemed like he was all-out pleading.

I hesitated, then said, "All right. Maybe."

"I'm taking that as a yes," Ruth said. "Let's meet outside the theater at five."

We spent the rest of lunch discussing whether or not to come to school in costume for Halloween on Monday— a definite no for me, since I'm allergic to people looking at me. Ruth was all over the idea though. She ran through her list of possible costumes, from Cruella de Vil to Rosie the Riveter. She apparently had a wardrobe that rivaled the Met costume gallery.

She snapped her fingers. "Oh, I have the perfect thing for you!" she said to Crud. "Picture this." She spread out her hands and waved them over Crud. "Black silk cape with red lining. Droopy hood."

"Vampire?"

"Vampire?! Please. No, I'm thinking sorcerer!"

Crud and I exchanged a quick glance of amusement, which Ruth caught.

"Okay, okay, I mean, it's not etched in stone or anything," Ruth said, misreading our expressions. "I also have a giant avocado costume that I'm pretty sure you could squeeze into."

4

THE FOUR-HEADED WEIRDO

The Last Chance Club met every afternoon in Room 101, which was the kindergarten classroom. Crud was already there when I arrived. He was standing by the glass aquarium tank, his arms folded across his barrel chest as he stared at a very fat hamster in the cage. It hadn't been there the day before.

"What do you think?" Crud squinted suspiciously at the hamster.

I crouched down and peered into the cage. The hamster waddled over to the plastic wheel and made a sad attempt to squeeze its pudgy body underneath it, only succeeding in tipping the wheel over.

"I think someone should ease up on its kibble."

"No, I mean do you think it's actually a hamster?" Crud asked.

"Ohhh!" I looked at Crud with wide eyes, realizing what he meant. "Right."

The last class pet had been a deranged Magician from the Nigh that Mr. Boot had turned into a ferret, so it wasn't out of the question that this hamster might be something other than a hamster.

I looked at it again more carefully. "Hard to tell," I said. "We can ask Mr. Boot."

Crud shook his head. "Boot didn't warn us that the ferret was really a Magician, did he? And that Magician almost dropped an apartment building on your head."

That was true actually.

"I have an idea." Crud unzipped his backpack and fished around in it. "There's this spell I've been practicing. . . ." He pulled out a thick book. It had a dark blue cover, and in gold lettering were the words *Last Chance Club Handbook, 112th Edition.*

"That thing is the size of a cinder block," I said.

"Yeah, I know. It's a beast. Every time I open it, there's, like, ten more pages filled with spells."

The club's handbooks grew on their own and at their own pace, depending on how skillful you were at magic. The better you became, the more spells it gave you. My handbook was about as thin as a comic book, a fact that definitely worried me.

"I've got loads of animation spells and illusion spells," Crud said. "Plus a bunch of protective wards and some weird spells too, like one that makes you grow a full beard in three seconds. I wouldn't mind getting one of those floating spells though."

"A spell that makes you float?"

"Nah, I have one of those. I'm talking about a spell that

floats from person to person. Only one person at a time is able to use it. Mr. Boot said they're really rare."

"I don't remember him talking about floating spells."

"I stayed late one time to get extra help with a protective ward and he told me about it then."

"Oh." I swallowed back my jealousy. I was an A student in all my classes. I mean, I barely even studied. But in the Last Chance Club, I was a disaster, a total brick.

"All right, let me see if I can find the spell I need. . . ." With a thud, Crud plunked his handbook on one of the tiny kindergarten desks and began to flip through the pages.

The door opened and Annika strode into the room. "Boot not here yet?"

I shook my head.

"So who do you think this special visitor is?" She flung her backpack on the ground. "Probably some weirdo freak. A guy with four heads and with legs like a rooster." Noticing that Crud hadn't even been listening, she turned to me. "What's with him?"

"He thinks Mr. Boot might have put the hamster under a spell."

"Like that ferret?" She walked over to the cage and looked at the hamster, who was now stuffing a baby carrot in its mouth.

"Hey!" Annika tapped on the glass and the hamster jerked its head up to look at her. "You hiding anyone in that hamster suit, Nibbles?"

"Here it is." Crud jabbed at a page in his handbook.

After studying the spell for a moment, he took out a pair of chopsticks from his backpack. The chopsticks were our "magic wands." Mr. Boot had explained that chopsticks were good at conducting magic, especially for beginners like us. That's because they're made of white spruce, a very snoozy type of wood that's only half awake (we had learned the hard way that even inanimate things were actually very much alive), so that the magic it produces is reliable. Very little chance of magical accidents.

Crud took the lid off the hamster's cage and gently scooped up the hamster. Holding it in the palm of his hand, Crud made several quick flourishes with his chopsticks. For a big lug of a guy, his movements were remarkably graceful and quick. In his hands, the chopsticks danced in the air, creating a spray of sparks that fizzled into smoky green vapor trails. It was a complicated spell, but Crud made it look effortless. It was no wonder his handbook was so massive.

"That's the Oofen Mumzer Spell." Annika nodded knowingly.

I guessed her handbook included this spell too. I felt a wave of dismay.

With a startled squeak, the hamster began to rise in the air, its little legs paddling, as though it thought it had suddenly been plopped into a swimming pool.

"How can you tell if Boot put a spell on him?" I asked.

"When you turn someone into an animal," Crud said, "they're tethered to a particular spot by a Shnoor."

"A Shnoor is a magical cord," Annika explained to me, which I resented very much. "Looks like tinsel."

"You really don't want to snap the Shnoor," Crud continued, "because then you break the spell, which means you might come face to face with something really nasty. So"—he glided his chopsticks to the right and the airborne hamster drifted to the right as well—"if we move the hamster to the outer edges of the Shnoor's reach, the Oofen Mumzer Spell will reveal the cord and we'll know if this little guy is under a spell."

"Better hurry up, Crud," I said. "If Boot walks in, he won't be happy about us snooping around his spell."

And of course, wouldn't you know it, at that moment the classroom door swung open.

Crud was so startled that he dropped his chopsticks, and the hamster dive-bombed to the ground.

"Oh no! No, no, no!" Crud cried out in anguish, crumpling to the floor beside the hamster. He put a hand on the little creature and, after a moment, choked out, "He's not breathing. I've killed him, I've killed him!"

It wasn't Mr. Boot who had entered the classroom, after all. It was a boy with a wild cap of curly hay-colored hair and thick black eyebrows. As he walked, there was a slap-slap sound from his left sneaker, the sole of which was partially detached. He was holding a purple plastic rectangular gadget with a digital display. Behind him were a bunch of other kids, all holding things that looked like defective science-fair projects—walkie-talkies wrapped in tin foil, a circuit board with wires hanging off it. One of them held a TV remote control attached to a Magic 8 Ball.

"We'll need to have a look around this room," the kid with the curly hair said officiously. He looked to be about ten at the most, and so skinny Crud could have snapped him like a pretzel stick. His voice was scratchy and high, so it sounded like it belonged to an old lady who had smoked for sixty years. Despite all this, he was clearly the leader of this ragtag group, who were bunched up behind him, peering into the room excitedly.

"Who are you clowns?" Annika stepped right up to the boy, arms crossed.

"That's not your concern," the boy answered.

I had to give it to the kid. If a girl who looked like Annika challenged most boys his age, they'd be reduced to a puddle of slobber. Not this kid. He acted like a hard-boiled police chief.

"Wait, I know who you are," Annika said. "You guys are the Boo Crew."

"What's the Boo Crew?" I asked.

"It's this nerd club that hunts ghosts," Annika explained. "You're Ben McElray's little brother, right?" she said to the leader. "Justin or Jarvis or something . . . ?"

"Jordan," he corrected. "And we're *paranormal investigators*." He held up his gizmo and waved it around the room while staring at the display. "My EMF detector is getting strong readings from this room."

I exchanged a nervous glance with Annika. Was it

possible this kid's Spook-O-Meter had picked up Crud's magic?

"This is a community service club. We do volunteer work," I told him. "There's nothing paranormal happening here."

Which of course was a big fat lie.

"All right, you guys, scram." Annika herded them out of the room, even as Jordan declared very dramatically, "The Boo Crew will be back! My detector doesn't lie!"

Once they were gone, I turned to Crud, who was still kneeling on the floor holding the hamster and sobbing.

"Are you sure he's dead?" I asked. "Maybe he's just in shock or something."

Crud shook his head. "He's dead. I killed him! *Stupid, stupid, stupid!*" He pounded his fist against his chest so hard I was afraid he'd crack his sternum.

"It's just a hamster, Crud," Annika said. "They have a lifespan of about ten minutes." Crud shot her a pained look.

"Unless," she added slowly, "it actually was a person who'd been turned into a hamster. Then I guess you could call it murder."

"Annika!" I hissed a warning, even though I realized she might be right. I turned back to Crud and asked, "Was it? A person?"

He shook his head. "I don't know. I hadn't finished the spell. I guess it could have been a person."

I noticed that the thought of having killed a person appeared to be somewhat less agonizing to him than the notion of having killed a hamster.

"If you killed someone that Mr. Boot put a spell on," Annika said, "he'll probably turn you into a crouton and toss you to a pigeon."

"Seriously, Annika, you're not making this any better," I warned.

"I'm just saying, Boot is not going to be happy about any of this. Neither is the four-headed weirdo with rooster legs."

"Do you think that Spook-O-Meter thing really picked up on our magic?" I wondered.

"I think it picked up on me," said a voice in the back of the room.

We all turned. Sitting in the rocking chair in the reading nook was a very thin teenaged boy with a mop of dark hair and sharp cheekbones. He was maybe eighteen or so and was wearing jeans and a pink T-shirt with a picture of a gaming controller, underneath which were the words, *I paused my game for this?*

The kindergarten room was not large. There was no way we wouldn't have noticed him. Yet none of us had.

"Where did you come from?" Annika asked.

"I've been sitting here all along. Watching you guys." He stretched his long legs out.

"Who are you?" I asked.

"I'm the four-headed weirdo."

5

TERRANCE

We barely had time to let this sink in, when the door opened again. This time it was Mr. Boot. Dressed in a dark suit, yellow tie, and carrying a worn brown brief-case, he walked briskly into the room but stopped short when he saw the teenager in the rocking chair.

"Ah. Terrance." Mr. Boot raised his hand in an awkward greeting. "Please excuse me for being late."

Annika and I exchanged glances. Mr. Boot was acting very strangely. In fact, he was acting as though he was scared, which was very un-Boot-like.

"No problem!" said Terrance cheerfully, exposing one crooked incisor. "It's given me a chance to get to know these fine youngsters."

Youngsters! The guy must have only been a few years older than us.

"Oh yes, yes, they're certainly . . ." He looked at us warily, as though he were trying to figure out just how much damage we had done in his absence. "They're a decent group of—" His eyes fell on Crud, who was still on the floor with the dead hamster in his hands.

"What's happened here?" Mr. Boot asked sternly. The old Mr. Boot had abruptly returned.

Crud got to his feet, his giant paws cupped around the hamster, and he opened his mouth to explain. But before Crud could get a word out, Terrance said, "Funny story about that."

Terrance hopped out of the rocking chair and sauntered over to Crud. He had a slump-shouldered, loose-limbed way of walking, as though he hadn't quite figured out how to manage his long arms and legs.

I held my breath for what would come next. If this guy had been sitting back there all along, he must have seen Crud put the spell on the hamster.

"Well," said Terrance, "it seems like this rabbit got caught—"

"Hamster," Crud corrected him.

"Oh sorry, it's been a while since I've been down here. Yeah, this hamster got caught under his . . . spinny whatchamacallit and he had a little shock."

Terrance took the hamster out of Crud's hands and studied the lifeless little thing. He puffed up his cheeks and gently blew on the hamster.

For a few seconds nothing happened. Then the hamster's hind legs kicked out. I watched in shock as it struggled to right itself, finally managing to sit back on its chubby haunches. Its pink paws swiped over its snout as it cleaned itself.

Crud, Annika, and I all gawped at Terrance. That hamster had 100 percent gone to the big toilet paper roll in the sky. And this guy, Terrance, had brought a dead hamster back to life.

Or possibly he had brought a dead person who had been turned into a hamster back to life.

"All better now, little . . ." Terrance frowned at the hamster, as though trying to remember what it was called again, and finally settled on, ". . . little animal thingy?" He handed the hamster back to Crud, who, dumbstruck, gently placed it in its cage, whereupon the hamster immediately grabbed a baby carrot and began eating.

"So!" Terrance clapped his hands. "Now that we're all acquainted, let's get down to business." He looked at Crud, Annika, and me. "I'm assuming Mr. Boot explained what's about to happen."

"Well, actually, I didn't have a chance to," Mr. Boot said hesitantly. "I only got word from the AOA this morning—"

"Seriously? *Gaaa!* That's on Fishbone. He's the new director, and between you, me, and the doorknob, he's not cut out for the job, but never mind. Yeah, so please, Mr. Boot, explain away." He bowed toward Mr. Boot, then stepped back and clasped his hands behind his back.

Mr. Boot cleared his throat. "As you know, the AOA is the Angelic Order of Alchemy. You may remember that I recently submitted your Last Chance Club handbooks to the AOA for inspection."

I did, and I had been mortified for them to see how few

spells I had in there compared to Annika and Crud.

"Apparently, the AOA was impressed with the amount of magic that had been added to your handbooks. As a result, they have issued each of you a learner's permit."

"Aren't we a little young to drive?" I asked.

"Not a driving learner's permit, Ms. Batista. The fact is, you three have been selected to be Watchers. It's an honor to be a Watcher." I saw Mr. Boot's eyes quickly flick over to Terrance, as though he were saying this for Terrance's benefit. "It's what we've been training you for. It's the reason why you have been learning magic in the first place."

"A Watcher?" Annika said doubtfully. "That sounds kind of stalker-ish."

Mr. Boot shot her a cautioning look. "Watchers have been around since the beginning of time. They make sure that things go the way they're supposed to go, for the good of everyone. Now that you'll be given learner's permits, you'll be able to accompany other Watchers and learn how—"

"Nope," Terrance interrupted.

"Pardon me?" Mr. Boot said to him.

"I mean, nope, they won't be accompanying other Watchers. They'll be given real, actual assignments."

"Are you saying that they'll be starting their Level Cs already?" Mr. Boot's voice was rising with real panic, which in turn made me start to panic.

"They'll be skipping right over the Level Cs actually.

They're going straight to the Initiation Trial."

"But no! That can't be!" Mr. Boot cried out in horror. "Watchers are trained for years before they're given the Initiation Trial. These children are not even remotely ready."

Terrance nodded in sympathy, his eyes flickering with concern toward the hamster. He'd seen firsthand that we were not exactly expert magicians.

"You don't have to convince me," Terrance said. "But the AOA seems to be fast-tracking them for some reason. And you can't argue with the AOA." Terrance shrugged. "Anyway, I've brought their gear—" Terrance walked back to the reading nook, where there were now three briefcases stacked on the floor beside the rocking chair. They hadn't been there before, I was almost sure of it.

"All right, let's see . . ." Terrance picked up the top brief-case. It was a mottled and scarred brown leather case with tarnished bronze studs along its edges and a bronze latch. Despite the fact that it looked like it had been kicked hard by steel-toed boots and then left outside during a hurricane, there was something dignified about it, as though it had been used for important business.

"This case is for Carmen Butterbank."

"That's me," Crud said. He walked up to Terrance and eyed the briefcase suspiciously before he took it.

The next briefcase was made of sleek maroon leather with gold hardware.

"This one belongs to Annika Rapp," said Terrance.

Annika marched up, grabbed the briefcase, and shook it.

"No, no! Please don't do that!" Terrance cried.

Annika shrugged and walked away.

"Last but not least . . ." Terrance picked up the remaining briefcase. It was very small and made of shiny white vinyl. "Nell Batista."

"Hey, Terrance," Annika said. "How come Nell's briefcase looks like a pretend nurse's kit for a six-year-old?"

"Hsst!" Mr. Boot warned her.

Leave it to Annika to say what everyone else was thinking. Anyway, I was pretty sure I knew the answer. I wasn't in the same league as Annika and Crud, and the AOA knew it.

"I'm sure Nell has everything she'll need in her briefcase," Terrance said, but as he handed it to me, his face was sympathetic. "Well." He rubbed his hands together. "I guess that's that. Oops, almost forgot this." He reached into his back pocket, pulled out an ivory-colored silk pouch, and handed it to Mr. Boot.

"But surely you can do something about this," Mr. Boot pleaded in a low voice as he took the pouch from Terrance. "It's not at all fair to them, you must see that."

Now I was getting really nervous. Because for the most part, Mr. Boot was not a fan of any of us. According to him, we were a sorry pack of troublemakers, and he would be only too happy to see the backs of us as soon as possible.

"They may surprise you, Luther," Terrance said. And

then . . . phttt! he was gone. He didn't dissolve or go out in a flash of light or anything like that. He just wasn't there anymore.

For a moment we all stared at the spot where he'd been standing, too shocked to say anything.

"Who was that guy?" Annika asked.

"An angel," Mr. Boot said grimly. "And not a very helpful one."

6

THE BREATH OF
FORBIDDEN KNOWLEDGE

"That dude in the gaming T-shirt was an angel?" Crud said to Mr. Boot.

"There are all types of angels, Mr. Butterbank."

"I can't open this thing." Annika was trying to work the latches of her briefcase.

"Your cases won't open until you use one of these." Mr. Boot pulled the drawstring of the silk pouch that Terrance had given him, extracted three cherry-red L-shaped devices, and handed one to each of us.

"It's an asthma inhaler," said Crud, as he examined his.

"You will place the short end in your mouth and press down on the canister."

"But I don't have asthma," Annika objected.

"Neither do I," I said.

"I used to have it as a kid—" Crud started.

"Oh for goodness sakes, will you all just do as I say," Mr. Boot cried wearily.

I put the short end of the inhaler in my mouth.

"I believe they've improved the flavor recently," Mr.

Boot said. "It used to taste of stewed beets."

I pressed down on the canister and a thin mist sprayed into my mouth. It wasn't bad actually. It tasted like a caramel had been vaporized and aerosoled.

"In a moment, you may feel slightly uncomfortable," said Mr. Boot.

That's when the pain hit. It felt like someone had poured salt straight into my veins. The burning sensation flooded my entire body, pinballing bursts of agony that started at the top of my head, moved to between my eyes, then slammed into my throat, my chest, working its way down. My entire body was trembling as it absorbed a level of pain that I'd never experienced before, and I bit down on my knuckles to keep from screaming. My eyes slid over to Crud. His heavy features were bunched up in a grimace, his thick dark hair drenched with sweat and plastered to his skin. Annika was also clearly in pain, but she was doing her best to control it. Her hands gripped the edge of her desk and her breathing was measured and deliberate, but her face was bloodless. I didn't have anywhere near Annika's self-control and I yelped out loud when I felt a staggering punch of pain at the base of my spine.

And then it was over.

Just like that, the burning sensation stopped. The pain vanished.

"*Slightly uncomfortable?*" Crud bellowed at Mr. Boot. He rubbed his sweaty forehead against his forearm. It looked like the pain had ended for him as well. "That's what you call *slightly uncomfortable?*"

"Would it have helped if I'd told you it would be excruciating?" Mr. Boot asked.

"What did you do to us?" Annika demanded. Her hands were no longer gripping her desk, but her face was still ashen. "What was that?"

"That was the Breath of Forbidden Knowledge. Each of you has just absorbed access to secrets that very few humans will ever know."

"Then how come I don't feel like I'm full of secrets?" Crud asked.

"For the most part, you won't notice any difference. However, should anyone in your immediate vicinity be in danger of making an unexpected choice that will alter important events in the future, you will be alerted. These unexpected choices are called Floopers, named for Fulvia Flupus, who changed the course of history by serving caraway seeds in her cabbage, which set off a series of events that led to the downfall of the Roman Empire."

"Seriously?" Annika said drily.

"When you are faced with a Flooper"—Mr. Boot ignored her—"you'll need to use all the magical skills I've taught you to ensure things happen the way they're supposed to happen. And you must be as inconspicuous as possible. You'll each need to successfully handle three Floopers to pass the trial. If you fail even one Flooper, you'll fail the entire trial."

"Won't people notice if we're performing magic spells on them?" Crud asked.

"People almost always find excuses for magic, Mr. Butterbank. Their brains simply won't allow them to notice it. Now, let's open up those briefcases and see what you're working with."

I opened the latches on my little white vinyl case. They weren't even proper latches, like the ones on Crud's and Annika's briefcases. They were those flippy latches that you find on metal lunch boxes.

Inside, strapped to the wall of my case with white elastic bands, were two small vials. Inside each vial was a tiny creature, no larger than a cricket. One of them looked like a crusty scab, with no other identifiable features except for a dozen or so filaments that sprouted from the center of the scab and waved around. Another one looked like an earthworm covered with tiny bristly quills like minuscule toilet bowl brushes.

"They're Fates!" Annika cried.

We had all worked with Fates before. They were creatures who lived in the Nigh, and though they were tiny, they were powerful. They were also, I was pretty sure, stolen from the Nigh and smuggled here—a shady little side hustle that I suspected Mr. Boot was involved in.

"Each of you will find information about your Fates and their operating instructions in your club handbook, as well as some information about Floopers." As soon as those words left Mr. Boot's mouth, we heard the *pffft* sound of pages being added to our handbooks. "You are to keep the Fates with you at all times. No exceptions."

"I've always wanted one of these things!" Annika cooed over her vials.

I peeked over at her briefcase. The sight of a dozen or so vials strapped into her briefcase's maroon silk lining made my stomach drop. Not only was I given the smallest case, I was clearly being shortchanged on the Fates as well.

Crud had as many, or more, vials as Annika, and from what I could see, their Fates looked a lot more interesting than mine—lively, humanoid little things, some with wings, glinting with a rainbow of opalescent colors.

"Fates are not *pets*, Ms. Rapp," said Mr. Boot. "And they don't belong to you. They're tools to be used for your Initiation Trial."

"They're not *tools*!" Crud said.

"Here we go." Annika rolled her eyes.

"Fates are living creatures," Crud said. "Living creatures that you've stuck in bottles!"

"Fates have a job, Mr. Butterbank. An important one. They shift events for the greater good of all. That's their purpose. And you will need them for the trial."

"Well, I'm not using them." Crud crossed his arms against his chest and sat back in his chair.

"Then you will fail your Initiation Trial," said Mr. Boot.

"Fine, then I'll fail," Crud shot back at him.

"And when you fail," continued Mr. Boot, "you will be kicked out of this club and expelled from school. That was the original a̱g̱ ꞏment, if you'll remember. It was the Last Chance Club or expulsion."

Crud tipped his thick chin up defiantly. "Then I'll be expelled."

"And the Umglick Spell will be performed on you so that any memory of this club and its members will be permanently wiped from your thick skull. You will not remember Ms. Rapp or Ms. Batista, and they won't remember you, except perhaps as a meathead who prowled the school hallways briefly before disgracing himself again."

This hit home. I watched Crud's face tighten.

"Does that go for all of us?" I asked. "If Annika or I fail, we'll be—"

"Yes, expelled," Mr. Boot said. "And your memories of everything that's happened here, and of each other, will be wiped clean."

I absorbed this, my stomach clenching with a sudden realization. . . .

"What about the Nigh?" I asked, my voice pitched with alarm.

I could tell by Mr. Boot's face that I was not going to like his answer.

"Should one of you fail, anything you three have experienced together will be extinguished from all your memories. Including the Nigh."

"So . . . we won't even remember it exists?" Annika asked.

Mr. Boot shook his head.

"But you would tell us, wouldn't you?" I said to Mr. Boot. "You would remind us and help us to get back there? So that we could get River out? River and all those other kids?"

"I'm also bound by rules. Immutable rules." Mr. Boot's voice was just above a whisper. His expression, usually so severe, softened to melancholy as he looked at all of us. "You three found your way to the Nigh accidentally. I didn't help you because I *couldn't* help you. Should one of you fail the trial, you'll have to find your way back again, which, I'll be frank, is highly unlikely."

"But that's not right!" I cried. "That's unfair!"

"Then the solution is simple." He took a breath, raised his chin. "Don't fail. Any of you. And incidentally"—he gazed around at us—"the hamster is indeed a hamster. In the future, please refrain from killing any more class pets."

7

A Kink in the Plan

Lately, Crud had gotten in the habit of walking me home from school, despite the fact that it was totally out of his own way. I was happy for his company, even when we walked in silence. There was something comforting about walking through New York City's streets with a kid who looked like he could put a rhino in a choke hold.

I had tried to stuff my little white briefcase into my backpack but, as puny as it was, it still wouldn't fit, so I had to suffer the embarrassment of carrying it.

"I've been wondering," Crud asked. "Why do you think the AOA fast-forwarded us?"

I looked around quickly before I answered. Through trial and error—sometimes painful error—we'd found if there was no chance of being overheard, we were able to talk about the club without having a streetlamp fall on us or some other freak accident.

"Probably because you and Annika are exceptionally good at magic. *Top of the class.*" I said this in a snooty British accent, which made me sound just as bitter as I felt.

"We're *all* good at magic, Nell. I was there when you did a pretty amazing Oifen Shoifen Spell in the Nigh, remember?"

"But it was easy to do spells in the Nigh," I complained. "The whole place was so highly charged that *he* could probably have done a decent Oifen Shoifen Spell in the Nigh." I nodded toward a shih tzu peeing on a tree. "But here, in this world? Okay, just look at this. . . ." I stopped walking, slipped my backpack off my shoulder, and unzipped it. I pulled out my handbook and gave it to him. "This past month I got only three new spells and they're all totally useless. One of them doesn't even have a name, and it did absolutely nothing when I tried it. Another one made things new again, but only for about three seconds. The last one I got was a total dud too. It said it was an 'interrupter spell,' whatever that is, and I practiced it until my fingers ached but still"—I shrugged—"nothing."

Crud flipped through the pathetically thin book, frowning.

"And don't try to make me feel better about it," I told him.

"I won't. This is pretty bad."

"Well, don't try to make me feel *worse* about it either!"

"Sorry. Have you asked Boot why you have so few spells?"

I nodded. "He just said that the handbook knows what it's doing. He said that magic governs itself and acts according to its own rules that we don't always understand and *blah, blah.* And now that stupid little briefcase? With only two pathetic-looking Fates? How am I supposed to stop the . . . the Floopers with this stuff? It's almost like the AOA knows I'm going to fail, so they're not even bothering. And, Crud, if I fail, what hope is there for River or for any of those kids stuck in the Nigh? If I can't remember the Nigh, I'll go back to believing that River is gone for good, or worse. . . ."

"I won't let you fail," Crud said. "Neither will Annika. We've all been through worse before. We can handle this."

"Thanks, Crud." I was touched by his words, but I still had this sinking feeling that Fate, or whatever you want to call it, was not looking kindly on me.

As we approached the bodega on Bleecker Street, I slowed down and checked the sidewalk for Chicken Bone Charlie, a local homeless person who had lived in the neighborhood for as long as I'd remembered. But the patch of pavement where Chicken Bone Charlie often sat, dressed in a filthy and tattered blue suit jacket, was empty. It had been for weeks now.

As kids we'd all been terrified of Chicken Bone Charlie, who would often chase us away from the bodega, waving a chicken bone at us as though it were a knife. Much more recently, though, I'd discovered that Chicken Bone Charlie was not at all who we thought he was. Chicken Bone Charlie wasn't even a guy. She was a woman named Mary Carpenter, and while she was homeless here, in the Hither—and admittedly not completely sane—she was a legend in the Nigh. Both a hero and a wanted criminal, she had helped to hide countless human children from the Magicians in the Nigh.

"Don't you wonder about Mary Carpenter?" I said. "Don't you think it's strange?"

"What is?"

"I mean, she was stolen by the Magicians and taken to the Nigh as a kid, just like River, just like all those other kids, right? And the Magicians forced her to use her mind to create things for them—to cast—skyscrapers and money and anything else they wanted, right?"

"Right."

"But when she escaped from them, she was able to come back home. She didn't get sick like all the other kids who tried to come home again. She didn't die. Why is that? What makes her different from them? What makes her different from River?"

"A fluke?" Crud suggested.

"I don't believe in flukes."

Out of the corner of my eye, I caught a flash of yellow and turned quickly, hopefully, to watch a taxi zoom by. It was just a regular taxi, though, and I let out a small sigh.

"I know what you're doing, Nell."

"What am I doing?" I tried to keep my voice as neutral as possible, but Crud wasn't fooled.

"You're looking for that taxi."

"What taxi?"

"What taxi?" He was getting good and annoyed now.

"Oh, I don't know, maybe the taxi that magically appears out of nowhere and takes people directly to the Nigh."

I opened my mouth to object, then stopped. I would feel like a dirtbag lying to him, and besides, he wouldn't believe me anyway.

"Okay, yes, I'm looking for *that* taxi," I admitted.

It was called the Anywhere Taxi, and we had taken it to and from the Nigh once before. It had stopped right in front of the bodega the last time, but I hadn't seen it again since, and believe me, I'd been checking several times a day.

"So let's say you see the Anywhere Taxi, what are you going to do?" Crud persisted. "Hop in and run off to the Nigh by yourself, with no help, no plan, and zero chance of coming back here alive? You may be smart and everything, but that is the stupidest idea I ever heard of."

"Yeah, well, what am I supposed to do?" I said, throwing up my hands. "Sit around and just wait for someone to figure out a way to bring my brother back home? And I don't know, Crud, it feels like I'm losing River more and more every day, like he just keeps drifting farther away, and now that note on the poster, and I just . . . I just can't keep waiting around."

"Boot says he's working on it."

"Boot says a lot of things," I grumbled.

"Okay, fine. Let's say you do see the Anywhere Taxi. You need a token to get to the Nigh. Do you have a token?"

"No." It was a kink in the plan, a major one.

"Right. So let's just wait to see what Boot comes up with, okay? In the meantime, we know that River is safe and that Tom is with him."

I nodded. That, at least, was a relief. We knew where River was hiding—a place called Elevator World. It had sprung from a story that River liked to tell me. He had been a masterful storyteller. He could spin tales out of thin air. Wild stories, but the way he told them, you just believed him. Maybe it was because he believed them. One of his stories was about a place called Elevator World, a place that was so real in our imaginations, River was able to cast it in the Nigh, and to hide there, where the Magicians couldn't find him. The fact that Tom went with him made me sleep easier most nights.

A man and a woman had walked up behind us, arguing in loud voices, which was a good excuse to quickly change the conversation.

"So why do you want me to go to the movies with you tonight?" I asked. It was actually something I had been wondering about. "I mean, aren't you and Ruth, like, a thing?"

"Hard to tell," Crud said.

"Wouldn't you know if you were a thing?"

There was silence as Crud lumbered along beside me, pretending to be suddenly fascinated by the store windows that we passed every single day. The conversation was obviously making him uncomfortable, but honestly, it was all so ridiculous.

Behind us the couple's argument was getting louder. He accused the lady of leaving her used dental floss on the bathroom sink while she brought up the fact that his toe-nail clippings were all over the house. From the sound of it, they were a perfect match.

"You know, Crud," I said, "you could just ask Ruth if she likes you."

"I can't just *ask* her that. It's not—it's not that easy."

"Why? Because she'll actually tell you?"

"Cold, Nell. Cold."

8

The Fates

D ad was in his workroom with the door shut, so I went directly into my bedroom. I sat down on my bed and placed the little white briefcase on my lap. Flipping the latches, I lifted the lid and instantly felt a slight belly squeeze of guilt at the sight of the two Fates trapped in those tiny vials. At least they didn't have faces. That made it somewhat easier.

"All right, let's see what you guys do."

Pulling out the *Last Chance Club Handbook, 112th Edition,* I flipped to the newly added pages at the end. The ink on the pages still looked shiny, as though it hadn't yet completely dried. At the top it said:

User Manual for Fates
BEGINNER'S KIT LEVEL 1 (Amateur/Dabbler)

Undidlier

CLASSIFICATION: The Undidlier is part of the Nulligan family of Fates, named for

Victor Nulligan, who created over four hundred styles of knots in his lifetime but was unable to untangle any of them. The Undidlier belongs to the subspecies Snarlcrackers.

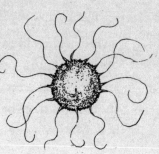

USAGE: Untangles knots. Also unfastens fasteners and unclips clips.

In the past, Undidliers were considered valuable household Fates, used to untangle tricky knots in shoelaces, knitting yarn, and rope. They were also used to loosen rusted bolts and unscrew the lids of jars. They were often kept as pets, housed in special cabinets built into the floors. Over the years, poor practices among Undidlier breeders have resulted in aggressive and uncontrollable progeny. Now considered to be a general nuisance, the Undidlier population is in decline due to the use of Undidlier glue traps and accidental smooshing.

Creeping Yeuk

CLASSIFICATION: The Creeping Yeuk is a member of the Botherations family, subgenus Super-Peevers

USAGE: Generates unreachable itches.

One of the oldest known Fates, fossil records
of the Creeping Yeuk have been found at
archeological sites of villages, indicating that
these Fates have been tormenting Folk since the
beginning of time.

I groaned. How was I supposed to pass the Initiation
Trial by making someone itchy or untying their shoelaces? I wondered what sort of Fates Crud and Annika had
received. I was pretty sure they were a lot better than the
crappy ones I was given.

I closed my handbook and bent down to tuck it into my
backpack again. That was when I noticed something moving on the floor.

My floor is painted to look like a pond with orange and
white speckled koi fish swimming in it. If you look closely
the marks on the koi fish are all shaped like things. One has
an orange heart on its head, another has a black key along
its spine, still another has a leaping black cat. My mother
painted the floor like this, not long before she walked out
on us. I don't remember much about her, just random useless things, like the fact that she liked to wear Dad's socks
and she could never find her wallet. She wasn't much of a
mother but she was a really good artist. The pond and the
fish on my floor looked so real that it sometimes made
you dizzy to walk across it. But now there was something
else on the floor too. A shadow, long and snaky, but also

vaguely human shaped. It looked as if it were swimming just beneath the surface of the painted pond, like someone trapped under ice. I held my breath, watching as the thing tested the corners of my room. It spun around and glided toward me, coming so close to my feet that I quickly swung them up onto the bed. My movement seemed to startle it. It hovered below me as I stared down at it. Something about it flagged me, a flash of a human face, its features obscured by a cloudy shifting shadow.

River?

My heart thumping, I leaned down, and the shadow lurched to the side in surprise. It could see me.

"River?" I said to it. "Is that you?"

The shadow shape began to glide closer again. There was something about its movements, something stealthy and cunning, which made me feel a sudden surge of fear. Whatever this thing was, it wasn't River.

Brrrrrr!

I jumped at the sound, smacking my head on the bottom of the upper bunk.

Brrrrr! Brrrrrrrrrrrrrr!

"Who is it?" I heard my father's voice.

Oh. Right.

The lobby buzzer.

When I looked down at the floor again, the shadow had vanished.

9

THE EXPERT ON EVERYTHING

A few minutes later I heard a knock on our front door, and then came a woman's voice, breezy and loud. And familiar: "Just look at the little fella! His head is smashed clean off his body!"

I opened my bedroom door and peered down the hall at a youngish woman with two braids, the tips of which were dyed acid green. Beneath a weathered army surplus jacket, she wore a purple dress that reached the tops of a pair of battered-looking hiking boots. She was hauling a lumpy backpack, sagging low on her back, and she held a pink ceramic something or other that was busted in two halves.

Vanessa Habscomb. Expert on everything, professional thief, and a pretty decent magician.

"Whaddup, Nell?" Vanessa said when she saw me. Her voice was cheerful enough, but her face looked unusually tense. I noticed a fresh pink scratch below her cheekbone with a slender thread of blood that hadn't yet coagulated. Caught beneath the strap of her backpack was a crooked twig with a single leaf, silver and luminescent.

She's just come from the Nigh, I thought. And it looks like she left in a hurry.

"May I see?" asked Dad, carefully taking the pink ceramic pieces out of Vanessa's hand.

He studied them, his dark eyebrows drawn together in his dusky, deeply creased face.

Dad handled valuable pieces of porcelain every day, painstakingly repairing cracks and chips until the pieces looked flawless again. This thing, however, was just a cheap ceramic pig, something you'd find in the FREE, TAKE IT PLEASE box at a yard sale. But Dad had compassion for all broken things. He held the pieces in the palm of his hand, rubbing his finger along the rough edge of the break thoughtfully, as if he were examining an injured bird.

"Not to worry, Vanessa, I'll fix him right up." He smiled at her. His face resembled one of the cracked vases he was always mending—full of spidery worry lines that had appeared soon after River went missing and had deepened each time I was tossed out of a new school. "Just give me a few minutes."

"Sure, sure, take your time," Vanessa said. "Anyway, I brought over a few old clothes of mine that I thought Nell might like." She patted her backpack and shot me a pointed look.

"Um, great," I said, taking the hint. "Let's go to my room and you can show them to me."

Once inside my bedroom, I closed the door and Vanessa plopped down on my bed, cross-legged. I sat down next to her, making a quick inspection of the floor. No shadow.

"Okay, here's the deal," Vanessa said in a hushed voice. "Some weird stuff is happening in the Nigh. Wickets are being destroyed, one after the other. It's like the whole place is being sealed off. Why? Dunno. And here's the other thing—these creatures are suddenly appearing in the Nigh. Creatures . . ." Vanessa lifted her upper lip, stuck out her tongue, and made her hands into T-rex claws that lunged at me. "Like blaaaah! Right? Really gnarly things that no one has ever seen before. I spotted one right before I leapt in the Wicket today. And listen, Nell, some of my sources are telling me that there's a chance—and this is what I really came here to tell you—there's a chance that the Magicians from the Nigh might, you know . . . come after you."

I took this in, feeling a rising chill of dread in my chest. "I think it's already happened."

I told her about the shadow while Vanessa listened, frowning.

"Ooo. Nope. I don't love the sound of that." She thought for a moment. "Hang on." She darted out of the room. I heard her footsteps hurrying down the hall, and then she returned a moment later. Sitting back down, she opened her backpack and pulled out a pair of chopsticks.

"Feet on the bed," she ordered.

I pulled my feet up and watched as she made several lightning-fast riffles with her sticks. There was a sudden odor of garlic bread in the air, and a second later my bedroom walls and floor began to glisten, as though they were freshly shellacked.

"Farzeenish Spell," she said. "I covered the whole apartment. That should keep out any Moss Necks, which is what I suspect you saw under your floor."

I reached out to touch the wall by my bed, but Vanessa swatted my hand away.

"That's a good way to lose a finger," she said. "You have to let it dry first."

"But what if Dad touches—"

"I checked on him before the spell. He's sitting on a stool, feet off the floor, hard at work on my little piggy. He won't notice a thing."

She was probably right. When Dad was doing repair work, he wouldn't notice if an actual two-hundred-pound pig waddled into the room. Already I could see that the shine was drying down and the walls and floor began to look normal again.

"Why are the Magicians after me?" I asked.

"Well, that's the thing we're not sure about. Maybe they think if they get their hands on you, they can force River to come out of hiding. The AOA always has a strong ward in place to prevent Magicians from the Nigh from coming into the Hither, but it's not foolproof. And the

Magicians can always send other nasty creatures that can slip right past a ward. Good thing I came when I did."

"But River's okay, right?"

"Oh sure. Yeah, he's safe as houses." Still, as she said this, Vanessa's eyes avoided mine. "It's you I'm worried about. And the Minister doesn't give up easily. I mean, yeah, you know that firsthand."

I did. It was only a few weeks ago when Crud, Annika, and I had a chilling encounter with the Minister, a pint-sized psychopath in tap shoes. She looked like a child, but River had warned us that she was very old, centuries old.

"So what am I supposed to do?"

"Don't do anything." Vanessa gave me a warning look. "I mean it, Nell. Don't try to fix this or I will personally kick your little booty."

"Fine."

"Mr. Boot and I are working on things from our end. Plus we have friends in the Nigh, spies who are watching out for any suspicious activity. In the meantime, do you have a brush?"

"A what?"

Vanessa reached out and quickly jiggled a hank of my hair.

"A brush. A hairbrush."

"O-kaay," I said doubtfully.

"And some hair ties."

I fetched a brush and the hair ties from my dresser

top and handed them to Vanessa. She gestured for me to turn my back to her as I sat down, and then she began to brush my hair.

"How is this supposed to—?" I turned around to ask, but she gave the crown of my head a quick slap.

"Stay still."

With her fingernail, she traced a line down the back of my head and separated my hair into two sections. Working quickly, she gave me two braids, just like the ones she always wore.

"Let's see." She turned me around by my shoulders and examined her work.

"Good." She nodded approvingly. She stuck her two pinkies in her mouth and let out a piercing whistle. There was a quick flicker by her ear and an incredibly tiny creature jumped onto her shoulder. It was man-shaped and pearl white with shots of pale pink opalescence glinting off spidery arms and legs. Attached to its back was a pair of membrane-thin wings. It looked an awful lot like a storybook fairy, but I knew that it wasn't. In fact, I'd seen a creature like this before, in the Nigh.

"It's a Willaweeper!" I said.

"His name is Winston." Vanessa stuck out her fore-finger and the little Willaweeper hopped on. It moved up and down her finger so rapidly, it was like watching someone dance under a strobe light.

Vanessa brought the little Willaweeper close to my

head and it leapt off her finger and onto my right braid.

"What's it doing?" I asked nervously, trying to see it side-eyed.

"Making himself comfortable. Willaweepers like to burrow between the twists of tree roots. He'll wedge himself between your braid and—*wooop*, there he goes!"

I felt several gentle tugs on my braid.

"What if I don't want him on my head?" I said. It gave me the heebie-jeebies, frankly. It was like having a grasshopper creeping through my hair.

"Oh, you'll want him there all right. It's basically like having a German shepherd on your head."

"Yeah, well, I don't want that either."

"No, see, Willaweepers are great at sensing danger before anyone else does. If Winston gets a whiff of a dangerous creature in the area, he'll start chirping in your ear. Best alarm system you'll ever have! It's how I'm able to keep myself out of trouble in the Nigh. Or mostly out of trouble, anyway."

I remembered that about Willaweepers. The one I had seen in the Nigh had sounded the alarm when a particularly terrifying creature had suddenly slithered up out of the underbrush.

I also remembered something else about Willaweepers.

"Wait. Don't Willaweepers like to pee on things?" I asked.

"Oh yeah." Vanessa nodded vigorously. "They're big pee-ers! But they only do it when they think something's funny."

"Great."

"Don't worry, you won't even know he's there."

"Unless he pees on me."

"Right. Then you'll know. Okay, off I pop." She stood up. "Oops, almost forgot." From her backpack, she pulled out a tangle of clothing that looked like it had been found under a park bench and she tossed it on my bed. "You know, in case your dad asks about the clothes. There's a yellow sweater that's pretty cute."

"Wait. Won't the Willaweeper just fly away?" I asked. I remembered the Willaweeper flying from tree to tree back in the Nigh.

"Nope. His wings are clipped." She made a little snip, snip motion with her fingers.

"But . . . that's so cruel!" I could only imagine what Crud would have to say about that.

"It doesn't hurt them," Vanessa replied defensively. "And how else are you going to keep a Willaweeper on you?"

I considered giving Winston back to her. It would be the ethical thing to do. It would be what Crud would have done.

"Their wings grow back," Vanessa assured me, seeing that I was hesitating. "And anyway, when it comes to flying, Willaweepers fly about as well as chickens do. Which is not very."

I weighed this against the fact that there might be all sorts of hideous creatures slithering out of the Nigh, with me as their target, and I decided that keeping Winston in my hair was probably a good idea after all.

Still, I was definitely not going to tell Crud about him.

10

PUMPKINS AND SKELETONS

After dinner, Crud met me outside my building so that we could walk to the movie theater together.

"What's with the . . . ?" Crud paddled his fingers below his ears, shooting me a befuddled look.

My braids.

I had already forgotten about them.

"Just trying something new," I said, attempting to sound casual and hoping the Willaweeper had concealed himself well enough that Crud wouldn't spot him.

When we hit West Thirteenth Street it began to rain, a spikey, cold drizzle. Neither one of us had brought an umbrella, so we just ducked our heads and walked faster. The Fates' vials were zipped into my jacket's inner pocket, my chopsticks were in my side pocket, and Winston was in my hair. I was as armed as possible for anything that the AOA or the Magicians threw at me—which, let's face it, probably wasn't going to be armed enough. I considered telling Crud about the shadow on the floor and what Vanessa had said—leaving out the

Winston part, of course—but he seemed hyper-nervous too. Whether it was because of the Initiation Trial or because of his sort-of date with Ruth, I wasn't sure, but we barely said a word to each other until we reached the Barton Theater.

There was a long line for tickets, and several of the people in line were in full creep costume, dressed in black suits and ties or 1950s-style dresses with pasty white makeup and black smudges around their eyes.

We found Ruth toward the back of the line, standing under an umbrella, another unopened umbrella in her hand. She was dressed in a yellow Morton Salt–girl–type rain jacket over a pair of swishy wide-legged pants. Her hair was parted severely to one side while the other side was pinned back with several chunky rhinestone barrettes—dressy for her, and a good this-is-a-date signal for Crud.

"You guys are going to love this flick," she said as she shifted the umbrella to cover my head and handed Crud her spare one. I could see Crud's face fall. I think he'd hoped to be the one sharing her umbrella.

"I'm smuggling a bag of bread sticks from the restaurant," she said, patting her rain jacket.

I glanced over at Crud, who looked glum beneath his umbrella.

"I'll grab us some drinks," I said. "Switch." I took Crud's umbrella out of his hands and gave him a nudge toward Ruth. He resisted, but she grabbed his elbow and pulled him close. He didn't fit all the way under the umbrella, but man did he look happy.

I had to walk a few blocks to find a place that sold drinks and finally settled on a little coffee shop. Once inside, I snapped my umbrella closed, spraying two girls sitting by the door, who both gave me the evil eye.

The whole place was decorated for Halloween. Candelabras suspended from the ceiling by fishing line, jack-o'-lanterns lining the top of the muffin counter. A life-sized plastic skeleton sat on a stool by the door, gripping a coffee cup in its bony hands.

I grabbed three sodas out of the open-air cooler and got in line to pay. In front of me was a tall blond man in a bulky green sweater.

"Soy pumpkin cinnamon latte with a shot of hazelnut and vanilla." The man in the green sweater gave his order to a barista who was a walking tattoo, wearing thick-framed glasses, large silver earplugs, a hoop through his nose, studs below his lips, and a silver barbell through his right eyebrow. "Oh, and whipped cream too, please."

The barista gave Green-Sweater Man an icy smile before he turned away to make the drink.

That was when I heard a voice say, "District Seven Dispatch."

I turned around to see who was talking. I figured there was a cop or an EMT behind me, but there was no one there.

I heard the voice again: "District Seven Dispatch with a Code 10-52 Flooper."

It was then that I realized the voice wasn't coming from a person; it was coming from inside my own head.

Oh.

The Initiation Trial was starting.

It was starting now.

With my heart kicking in my chest, I listened as the voice continued:

"Target is male, blond hair, tacky green sweater. Nose bears striking resemblance to a wedge of mozzarella cheese. Please stand by."

"Oopsie, I forgot to say caramel drizzle," Green-Sweater Man called to the barista's back before turning to me, grinning sheepishly, and stage-whispering, "I think that barista hates me."

Blond hair. Check.

Tacky green sweater. Check.

Nose like a wedge of mozzarella cheese. Yup.

"Do not let target leave the store." The dispatcher's voice was more urgent now. "Repeat, keep the target in the store until clearance."

"How am I supposed to stop him?" I whispered this out loud, but either the dispatcher was ignoring me or else this was a one-way communication, because she didn't respond.

I took out my phone to text Crud for backup.

"To stay or to go?" the barista asked Green-Sweater Man.

"To go."

Okay, no time to get Crud here. Think, think!

The barista plunked down the man's drink on the counter. "Soy pumpkin cinnamon latte. Shot of hazelnut and vanilla. Whipped cream. Caramel drizzle." He announced each ingredient with a snarl of disdain.

"It's actually delicious," Green-Sweater Man assured the barista as he pulled a card out of his wallet and shoved it in the reader.

Panicking, I unzipped my jacket's inner pocket and pulled out the first vial I touched. Without even checking to see which one it was, I removed the stopper. Something flew out of the vial so fast that I only caught the quickest glimpse of it. It looked like a microscopic jellyfish with its threadlike silvery filaments waving in the air. If you weren't looking for it, you might have mistaken it for a stray dust mote. Or a floating scab.

The Undidlier flew around over our heads until I lost track of it, but suddenly there was a plink sound. Something small and shiny dropped on the checkout counter, seemingly from nowhere.

The barista looked down at it, confused.

Plink, plink, plink.

Shiny beads and tiny hoops appeared to be raining down on the counter from above.

"They're from your"—Green-Sweater Man wiggled a finger at the barista—"from your face."

The silver barbell slipped out of the barista's eyebrow and landed on the counter.

Plink!

The Undidlier was undoing the barista's piercings one by one.

Plunk! Plunk! His earplugs fell out.

With no piercings and his thick-framed glasses, the barista now resembled an IT guy with gross, stretched-out earlobes. Clearly mortified, he quickly scooped up his studs and hoops and earplugs and tucked them in his apron, which was now untied and hanging loosely. The Undidlier's handiwork, no doubt.

"That'll be five seventy-eight," the barista muttered.

The minuscule Fate floated back over to me. I caught it and deposited it in its vial. All in all, the Undidlier had only managed to buy me an extra minute and half.

I'd have to think of something else.

Green-Sweater Man's finger was hovering over the button that asked if you wanted to leave a tip.

I knew some spells, but not many. The problem was that they would only work with a decent Oomphalos, which this café did not seem to have. An Oomphalos is a spot where energy converges and makes magic possible. In the Nigh, a powerful Oomphalos lingered in the air all the time, like oxygen molecules. But here, back home, a really great Oomphalos was hard to find. It seemed to work like a phone signal—stronger in some spots than others. In the café, all I felt was a very subtle hum of energy. It wasn't nearly enough for any real magic, but maybe I could manage to do something.

I looked around the room until I spotted the skeleton

sitting on the stool by the door. I could try the Oifen Shoifen Spell. It was a spell that animated moderately sleepy things like plastic, so it was worth a shot. Grabbing the chopsticks out of my coat pocket, I performed the Oifen Shoifen Spell as swiftly as possible. The results were underwhelming. All it did was make the skeleton twitch the slightest bit, just enough for the two teen girls sitting nearby to glance at it, widen their eyes, and giggle.

Green-Sweater Man was on the move now, heading for the door.

"*Detain immediately. I repeat, detain immediately!*" the dispatcher shouted in my head.

I shifted to the right, where I could feel a slight strengthening of the Oomphalos. I tried the Oifen Shoifen Spell once more, making sure my movements were as sharp and crisp as possible. Green-Sweater Man had nearly reached the door when the skeleton pitched forward. The coffee cup it held in its boney hands plopped to the floor.

That was it. Pretty lame. Still, it made Green-Sweater Man pause and look down at the cup that was rolling across the floor by his feet. That's when he noticed that his shoelaces were untied.

The Undidlier.

Right.

Green-Sweater Man placed his coffee on the window ledge by the skeleton, knelt down, and began to tie his shoes.

Outside, right in front of the café, something huge and orange fell out of the sky, crashed down on the pavement directly in front of the café with a *thwack*, and smashed to smithereens.

Everyone in the café stopped talking. We all stared out at the thing, which was now splattered all over the sidewalk.

"It's a pumpkin," one of the teen girls said in amazement.

"It's a *monster* pumpkin," the other girl said.

Green-Sweater Man peered through the glass door. "That thing must weigh two hundred pounds. One more second, and I would have been right under it." He looked around at all the stunned faces in the café. "Imagine . . ."

"*Target cleared for exit*," the dispatcher said. "*Flooper successfully neutralized.*"

By the time I got back to the theater, Crud and Ruth had already bought the tickets. They were standing together under the umbrella, talking and laughing. At least, that part of my plan had gone smoothly.

The moment Crud caught sight of me, his smile dissolved. I probably still looked all jaggedy from what had just happened. I'd managed to avert disaster, both for Green-Sweater Man and for me, but it had been a close thing. Too close. My legs were still trembling and I had a death grip on the chopsticks in my pocket.

It wasn't until after we had found seats and Crud and I

volunteered to go fetch some candy that I had a chance to tell him what had happened.

"A pumpkin?"

"Not a regular pumpkin, Crud. This thing was a mutant pumpkin! Apparently it was for a Halloween party on the roof. If I hadn't stopped that guy from leaving the café, he would have been puree."

"You did stop him, though." Crud turned to the guy at the snack counter. "Pixy Stix."

"I stopped him by the skin of my teeth. And I don't know about your teeth, but mine don't have any skin."

After the whole harrowing experience in the café, the last thing I needed was to watch a movie about a woman who's the victim of a deadly accident and is then haunted by ghouls. The second to last thing I needed was to watch the movie while people dressed as ghouls roamed the aisles and shrieked in my face.

And there was something else too.

The first time some goon in stage makeup sidled up the aisle, poked his face close to mine and screamed, I felt warm liquid dribble onto my lap. I thought that the guy in the costume must have spit on me as he was scream-ing. But when a girl ghoul waved her hands in my face and screamed, "They're everywhere! They're everywhere!" I felt another warm liquidy dribble fall on my lap.

Then I remembered.

Winston.

Apparently Winston thought those screaming ghouls

were absolutely hysterical, because every time one of them came near, he would pee on me. All in all, it was not exactly a fun night out for yours truly.

"See, kid," Ruth said once the movie was over and we were out in the lobby. "That wasn't so bad."

"Yeah," Crud agreed, "the movie was more stupid than—" He had stopped talking and I followed his gaze down to my leg, where splotches of wetness darkened my jeans.

"That's not . . ." I sputtered. "I didn't . . ." I couldn't tell them about Winston, obviously.

Ruth hooked her arm around my shoulders. "True story, I once peed my pants when I met Big Bird at *Sesame Street Live.* It happens to the best of us, kid."

11

STREET FAIR

The following morning, I woke up to a knock on my bedroom door.

"Yes?" I croaked sleepily.

My dad poked his head in. "Um, you have visitors."

I squinched my eyes open, but shut them again, ambushed by a pillar of light coming through the busted venetian blinds.

"Who?"

"Annika," Dad said. "And some boy named Grub."

"It's Crud," I heard Crud call from behind him.

I sat up as Annika squeezed past my dad, with Crud in her wake. Annika was carrying her briefcase but Crud wasn't.

"It's okay, Dad," I said.

He nodded, worriedly eyeing the thuggish-looking Crud before closing the door.

Annika was dressed in a black military-cut jacket and a red scarf. Her hair was piled up in a bun and secured by her chopsticks. With her maroon suitcase, she looked like a very young businesswoman. Or maybe a CIA operative.

It was strange to see her in my room again after all these years. When she was a little kid, she lived in the apartment next door to us and came over to play all the time. She was River's friend, not mine, not really. I had never really liked her much back then. I'm pretty sure the feeling was mutual.

Annika must have felt the oddness of being in the room again too, because she had opened her mouth to say something, then stopped. She looked at the upper bunk—River's bed. His old quilt was still on it, neatly smoothed. Untouched since he'd gone missing.

Her face softened and I saw her throat tick with a swallow.

"We like to keep it the way it was," I told her.

I had caught her out and she didn't like it. Her face regrouped back into its usual cool expression. "Crud told me that you almost tanked your trial yesterday. Nice going."

"That's not exactly what I—" Crud started.

"Anyway," Annika continued, "there's a street fair today on Eighth Street. Loads of people, which means loads of potential Floopers. If we all work together, we can pass this stupid trial. Terrance didn't say that we couldn't team up, and let's face it, if we try to do this on our own, it's going to be a disaster. I mean, I'll be okay, but this dummy"—she jerked a thumb at Crud—"refuses to use his Fates."

"Oh, so I'm a dummy because I actually have a heart?" Crud objected.

"That's right," Annika replied. "And you"—she nodded

at me—"are working with spit and fumes. If one of us fails, we'll all fail. And guess what? I'm not failing. So get your butt out of bed, Anne of Green Gables, and let's do this."

"Anne of Green Gables?" I repeated in confusion.

"Your—" Crud pointed to my head.

Oh.

I touched my braids. I'd forgotten they were there. Hopefully the Willaweeper was still tucked inside them and I hadn't rolled over and smooshed him in my sleep.

"I'm just trying something new," I muttered in an effort to explain the braids.

"Yeah? Well, new isn't necessarily better," Annika said before they left me to get dressed.

I don't know what it is about street fairs that turns seen-it-all, done-it-all New Yorkers into a bunch of wide-eyed bumpkins. People roamed the length of Eighth Street, gawking at stalls filled with junk that they wouldn't have looked at twice in a regular store, all the while eating things like bacon jalapeño corn dogs and pizza sticks.

Annika was right—the street was so packed that we had barely passed the third stall before Annika stopped walking and pointed at her head.

"Incoming Flooper," she said.

Crud and I waited while she listened.

"Dispatch says the target is a lady to our left. Stocky, black hair, looks like a mustard jar."

We all scanned the crowd to our left.

"There!" Crud pointed to a lady with a short cap of black hair who was wearing a boxy, bright yellow peacoat.

"Dispatch is rude," I said.

"Dispatch is accurate," Annika replied. "That lady does look like a mustard jar. Hang on, Dispatch is talking again." Annika listened. "She says the target needs to head over to the blooming onion truck pronto. It's a Code 10-78."

Crud nodded knowingly.

"10-78?" I asked. "What's a 10-78?"

"The codes were in our handbooks," Annika said. "Didn't you memorize them?"

Actually, I had noticed a list of codes after the descriptions of my Fates, but I had been so distracted by the shadow on my floor, and then Vanessa's news, that I hadn't gone back to look at them more closely.

"I'm assuming that's a no," said Annika drily when I didn't respond.

"A 10-78 is a Romantic Intervention," Crud explained.

"In other words, a 'meet cute,'" said Annika.

This assignment sounded a whole lot less treacherous than preventing a two-hundred-pound pumpkin from landing on someone's skull.

"Blooming onion truck's back that way." Crud pointed in the direction we'd just come from.

"Okay." Annika lifted one knee, balanced her briefcase on it, then started to open the latches to retrieve one of her Fates. "This will be easy."

"Hang on! I've got one too," Crud said suddenly. As he

listened to the dispatcher's instructions, a look of dismay passed over his face.

"It's a Code 10-23 at the tarot booth." Then for my sake, he added, "Code 10-23 is Information Manipulation. Dispatch says I have to change the cards that the reader pulls." He let out a low growl of dismay. "Tricky one."

"I told you you'd need your Fates!" Annika cried. "You should have brought your briefcase."

"I can do this without the Fates," he insisted, but I could tell he wasn't totally confident.

And then, at the worst possible moment, I heard a voice in my head. "*District Seven Dispatch.*"

"No, not me too!" I said.

"Flooper?" Crud asked.

I nodded.

"Can't these people handle their own lives?" Annika said.

"*District Seven Dispatch with a Code 10-81,*" I heard in my head.

"What's a Code 10-81?" I asked them.

Annika frowned at Crud, who looked baffled.

"Oh no. What is it?" I asked.

Crud shook his head. "I don't know. That wasn't on the list of codes."

"*Target is behind you,*" I heard the dispatcher say. "*Young male, eleven years old. His hair looks like there was an explosion in a ramen noodle factory. Eyebrows like someone slapped two pieces of electrical tape on his forehead.*"

I turned around and sure enough, the boy was standing a few feet behind me. Not only that, I knew him. Those thick black eyebrows pinched together as he gazed down at his Spook-O-Meter. It was the kid from the Boo Crew. Jordan.

12

SKULL 'N BONES

"Target must not enter Skull 'n Bones," the dispatcher said. "Repeat, this is a Code 10-81."

"What did she say?" Crud had been watching my face carefully.

"It's about that Jordan kid, from the Boo Crew." I nodded toward him. "I'm supposed to keep him away from Skull 'n Bones."

"Isn't Skull 'n Bones that store on Astor Place?" Annika asked.

"It's the only place I know with that name."

"Okay, we'll have to split up," Annika said. "Crud stays with me."

"Why with you?" I cried.

"Because I'm faster at the spells than either of you and he's going to need speed for his Flooper. You just need some ammo." You could see Annika's mind strategizing like an army general. "You'll need one of my Fates because your Fates are clearly trash." She looked in her briefcase and examined the vials, tapping her nails on the glass.

"Stop that!" Crud said. "You're scaring them."

I turned to check on Jordan. He was on the move, heading up the street toward a crowd of people watching a bagpiper playing heavy metal music.

"I have to go, Annika. I'll lose him!"

"Relax, will you?" Annika chose a vial and handed it to me. "This should do the trick."

"I'm going with her," Crud told Annika.

"No, you're not. Not unless you want to fail your trial. Nell can handle this, Crud. She's a decent magician and can do better animation spells than either of us."

Annika's words shocked me and frankly gave me a jolt of confidence. Maybe that's just what good generals do before they send their soldiers off to get smoked in battle, but it worked.

I closed my fist around the Fate's vial and ran, plowing through the crowd, leaving a wake of annoyed New Yorkers whose comments were thankfully drowned out by the bagpipes. Up ahead, I spotted a mop of pale brown noodlish curls. Jordan was ambling along, his eyes glued to the ridiculous Spook-O-Meter. Look, I'm the last person who should be making fun of things like ghost hunting, but seriously? The device looked like something he'd built from a kit. Still, Jordan definitely seemed to think he was on the trail of something. He kept weaving slowly from one side of the street to the other as he watched the Spook-O-Meter.

Skull 'n Bones was at the end of the street, on the

corner. I'd been in the store a few times. It was both gross and fascinating, with displays of pig skulls and stuffed badgers, preserved alligator heads and baby sharks bobbing in canisters of blue liquid. The whole place smelled of incense and formaldehyde, like a witch doctor's pharmacy.

I caught up with Jordan, staying a few yards behind him so as not to tip him off. He stopped short near a tube socks vender and held up the Spook-O-Meter, moving it around slowly as though he were trying to catch a signal. I pretended to examine a spindle full of socks embroidered with tiny tacos, then opened my hand to examine the glass vial that Annika had given me.

Standing in the vial was a tiny man wearing a weedy tunic. He had a craggy face, but his body was long-limbed and muscley. In one tiny hand he held an impossibly thin stick.

"You're a Whirdle!" I whispered with delight. I knew about Whirdles. Mr. Boot had shown us how to use them a while back.

I pulled the stopper off the Whirdle's vial and carefully tipped the vial over my hand. The Whirdle sprang out onto my palm. He bounced the stick lightly against his hip, his legs bent and joggling up and down, ready for action. He looked up at me, which gave me a gut-squeeze of guilt. Unlike the Undidlier, the Whirdle had an actual face, with eyes and a mouth and everything. I thought about what Crud would say, and I almost caved, but then I remembered the consequences if I failed.

I edged closer to Jordan, feeling the air for an Oomphalos I could work with. For once, I'd lucked out. There was a nice buzzy Oomphalos right near the sock spindle. Leaning down, I pretended to scratch my shin and I dropped the Whirdle on the top of Jordan's right sneaker. The Whirdle was so tiny that a person would have had to really look for him to notice he was there. I watched as the Whirdle scrambled to his feet, his legs straddling either side of the sneaker's tongue. Grabbing the laces like reins, he stood there, waiting.

Right. Now I had to animate Jordan's shoes.

I stuck my hand in my coat pocket and took out my chopsticks. As swiftly as possible I performed the Ver-blunget Spell—a somewhat tricky spell that meshed elements of the Oifen Shoifen Spell with mentally repeating the directional coordinates. It took me a minute to decide, but I figured "one block east, one block south" should keep Jordan well away from Skull 'n Bones.

It was a spell Mr. Boot had made us practice a few times during club hours, but I was still amazed when it actually worked. Jordan's sneakers stamped at the ground suddenly, the semidetached sole of his left sneaker snapping against the pavement double-time. Jordan shifted his attention from his Spook-O-Meter to his out-of-control feet, as though he had tripped on something. At that instant, the Whirdle began to whip Jordan's sneaker with his stick. Jordan's feet made an abrupt pivot and Jordan began to walk in the opposite direction of Skull 'n Bones while I stayed close behind. The Whirdle was driving Jordan's shoes like a jockey on a horse, forcing him to weave through the crowds until the Whirdle stopped him in front of a food truck selling fried dough.

Jordan looked up at the menu painted on the side of the truck, as though he'd been planning on getting some fried dough all along. Mr. Boot had been right—people almost always find excuses for magic. Their brains just flip things around to turn the magic into something everyday-ish. That's why they don't notice magic when it happens to them.

I was just about to text Crud to give him an update, and to see how he and Annika were doing, when Jordan suddenly lurched away from the fried dough line. He was staring at the Spook-O-Meter again, which was now flashing red. I crept closer to see if the Whirdle had fallen off his sneaker, but no. The little guy was still there, smacking Jordan's shoe furiously. Apparently, Jordan had a will of steel, because he ignored the Whirdle's efforts and started making his way back in the direction of Skull 'n Bones. Every few steps he stumbled, no doubt the result of fighting both his magically animated shoes and the Whirdle. After a particularly bad stumble, which almost landed him nose-first on the pavement, Jordan stopped walking. I thought he would turn around, but no. He crouched down and wrenched both his sneakers off his feet. I guess he thought he was tripping because of his one messed-up sneaker. You had to admire his determination. Walking in your socks in New York City is hard-core. The poor Whirdle was thrown from the sneaker and landed on the sidewalk, right in the path of a woman whose chunky heels just missed crushing him. I rushed in, scooped him up, and deposited him safely back in his vial. Crud would have had a heart attack if he'd witnessed that.

Now that the sneakers were removed from Jordan's feet, the Verblunget Spell was broken. The sneakers, which Jordan held by their laces, dangled as though exhausted.

Skull 'n Bones was dead ahead. At the rate he was walking, Jordan would be there in a matter of seconds.

"Situation approaching critical," I heard Dispatch say. "Divert target immediately!"

I took off at a sprint, treading across a chalk sidewalk drawing in progress. The artist, a teenager in a red hoodie, wailed in protest. Reaching the store a moment ahead of Jordan, I did the only thing I could think of. It wasn't elegant. It wasn't even magic, and I was pretty sure it was breaking some sort of AOA rule. I stood in front of the doorway of Skull 'n Bones, spread my arms wide, and blocked Jordan's way.

"I need to get in there," Jordan said, his eyes darting between me and his Spook-O-Meter.

"Nope."

The chalk artist in the red hoodie had been watching us, and now he got to his feet and was heading our way.

"Hey, leave the little kid alone!" the chalk artist demanded as he approached. "Let him go in the store if he wants."

"This is no joke," I told Jordan. "You need to go play somewhere else."

It was the wrong thing to say. Jordan got all puffed up and red in the face. "*Playing?* You call investigating the deepest mystery of humankind *playing?* See this?" He shoved his Spook-O-Meter in my face. There was a spectrum of green to red bands on the thing and the light above the last band was flashing quickly. "This is the highest reading I've ever gotten. There is something in that store, something important, so . . . Get. Out. Of. My. *Way!*"

He pressed his hands against my left shoulder and tried to push me aside, but he was astonishingly weak. He was huffing and grunting with the effort, and honestly, it would have been funny if Dispatch hadn't started shouting in my brain, "*Divert, divert, divert!*"

And then I heard something else.

"*Wickle-wickle-feee! Wickle-wickle-feee!*"

It wasn't coming from Dispatch; the sound wasn't coming from inside my head. It was coming from right next to my ear. It took me a second to realize what it was.

Winston! The Willaweeper had wedged itself so

snugly in my braid that I had forgotten it was even there.

"*Wickle-wickle-feee! Wickle-wickle-feee!*"

I knew that sound. I had heard it once before, in the Nigh, just seconds before one of the most horrifying creatures I'd ever seen in my life slithered out of the underbrush.

Now, once again, a Willaweeper was sounding the alarm.

I fought back panic, planting my feet against Jordan's efforts while scanning the street for signs of something, though what exactly, I wasn't sure. I knew, from painful experience, that the Nigh harbored all sorts of dangerous creatures, but would they appear in broad daylight in the middle of lower Manhattan?

The chalk artist had grabbed the sleeve of my jacket and seemed ready to wrench me away from Jordan when from somewhere behind me I heard a woman scream. I swiveled around, and to my horror, I saw that a cab was driving the wrong way down the street. It jumped the curb and barreled directly at us at an alarming speed. It all happened so fast that I simply froze on the spot and shut my eyes, bracing myself for the impact. There was a deafening screech, and when I didn't feel two tons of metal slamming into me, I opened my eyes to find that the cab had stopped inches from my body. Jordan had ducked out of my suddenly loosened grip and was now pulling open the door to Skull 'n Bones. I made a lunge to stop him, but at that moment the cab's back door swung open and a boy with egg yolk–colored hair grabbed my arm and pulled me into the backseat.

"Take us to the Nigh!" he called to the taxi driver as he slammed the door shut.

13

Anywhere Taxi

Under any other circumstances, I would have been thrilled to see this particular boy. I mean, I would have been spewing actual rainbows. But right now, I just wanted to strangle him.

"You seriously have the *worst* timing on the planet!" I cried.

"I have the *best* timing," he answered, grinning and flinging his arms across the back of the cab's seat in a very self-satisfied way.

That's how Tom is. Overly confident and so cheery about it that it's hard to get mad at him. But not this time. This time he had completely botched things up.

"You don't understand! I . . . There was . . ." I was so mad, I was sputtering. "There was this kid and I had to keep him out of that store and now he's in there—"

"I know all that, Nell," Tom said, waving off my explanation. "Why do you think I grabbed you?"

"But I could have stopped him!"

Tom shook his head. "You were never going to stop him."

"You don't know that."

The cab hadn't moved, not an inch. Still, the cabdriver, a man with a shoulder-length mane of silver hair beneath a yellow cap with a shiny black brim, glanced at me in his rear-view mirror and in a bored voice said, "Welcome to the Nigh." His eyes narrowed at me in the mirror. "Hey, ain't you been in my cab before?"

I nodded.

"I don't think I liked you."

"Probably not."

"All right . . . out, the both of you." The driver jerked his head toward the passenger door.

Through the window on the driver's side, I could see people in the street outside Skull 'n Bones, gawping at the taxi, and behind them, in the distance, was the blue and red flash of a police car heading our way. Out of the passenger side window, however, the view was entirely different: a barren, wild-looking scrap of land, shrouded in fog. The Anywhere Taxi straddled the two worlds, one half in the Hither and the other in the Nigh.

Tom opened the passenger side door and hopped out. I hesitated, weighing my options. I'd failed my trials. Once they performed the Umglick Spell, I'd lose any memory of pretty much everything I cared about. On the other hand, I was here, in the Nigh, a place I'd been trying unsuccessfully to get to for weeks.

The cabdriver whipped his head around and barked at me, "I said OUT!"

I scooched straight out of the Anywhere Taxi, on the passenger side. The second I stepped foot on the ground, the taxi vanished.

The streets of lower Manhattan were gone. Instead, we stood on a rocky patch of beach.

Directly in front of us was a wooden sailboat, tip-tilted, propped up against the side of a tree at the base of a low bluff. It was an odd-looking boat with peaks on either end. Patched here and there, it looked like it had seen better days. It had a single, worn-looking mast that was strung with heavy rope and a furled sail. Hanging from one of the pointed ends of the boat was a green cap with brown fur around its rim. Tom's Viking hat.

I assumed there was water nearby because I heard the hish-hish of waves breaking on the shore, but a heavy fog completely concealed everything beyond the borders of the banks.

Tom scrambled up the tree and leapt onto the boat's deck.

"So what do you think?" He smiled down at me and raised his arms to indicate the area all around us.

"What is this place?" I asked.

"It's where I live."

I'd never actually considered where Tom's home was. If I pictured him anywhere, it was out at sea, on the prow of a ship, his sun-pinched blue eyes fixed on the horizon.

Looking around, I could see the land rise up from the rocky banks to a scrubby sweep of wild grasses. Apart from the sound of the waves, the place was completely, utterly silent.

"Where's River?" I asked.

Tom's smile faded.

Uh-oh.

I felt a ball of fear forming in my gut.

"*Where's River?*" I repeated.

"I don't know."

"How can you not know? I thought you were going to stay with him!"

"I *did* stay with him," he insisted. "It was River who left."

"What are you talking about?"

Tom crossed his arms and sighed heavily, his shoulders heaving.

"We had gone to this place in Elevator World with all these really tall trees and a bridge that connected the tree-tops, one to the other. And you could walk on the bridge for miles."

I nodded. I knew the place he was talking about. It often turned up in River's stories.

"So we were sitting on the bridge, high up in the trees, with the birds flying all around us. River had been acting weird for a few days. Really quiet, like he was thinking about a problem he just couldn't figure out. Then he said to me, 'I can't hide forever, Tom. You know that, right?' And I said sure, I know that. I told him that people were going to find a way to get him home again, that Mr. Boot was working on it, but he kept saying, 'I have to do something, Tom, I can't just sit around and wait.' And the next day he was gone."

I let this sink in. I had said something very similar to Crud yesterday.

"Listen, Nell, Vanessa has been out looking for him, and—"

"Vanessa! She knew River was gone? She lied to me."

"Yeah, well, she was afraid you'd try and go looking for him yourself. That's why she asked me to keep an eye on you. She even persuaded the Anywhere Taxi driver to let me follow you around this morning and everything."

"I can't believe Vanessa didn't—" I felt a sudden pinch on the side of my neck and I swung around in time to see a gossamer figure behind me, shifting uneasily. It was as though there was a rip in the air in the shape of a small human figure, through which a nimbus of light and dust shone.

"I saw that, Katerina!" Tom pointed at the figure.

As the small form glided backward, I thought I could make out the likeness of a face, glaring at me sullenly. I turned back to Tom.

"What is—"

"Come on." Tom grabbed his Viking hat and jammed it on his head. Then he leapt off the boat, straight to the ground, as light-footed as a panther. He took my hand in his and, I'm not going to lie, my brain instantly liquefied.

"Wait!" I shook my hand loose and squinched my eyes

closed for a second, trying to stay focused. "Back in the taxi, you said I was never going to stop Jordan from going into the store. How do you know that?"

Tom sighed, as though I were spoiling his fun. He flung himself on the ground and stretched out, crossing his ankles and putting his hands behind his head.

"Red hoodie."

"What?" I sat down on the ground beside him. "You mean that kid who was doing chalk drawings?"

Tom turned on his side to look at me, crooked his elbow and rested his head in his hand. "Not a kid. An Imp. A dangerous one. He was waiting by that store."

"Why?"

"Who knows, but you can be sure it wasn't for anything good."

"The Willaweeper!" I touched my right braid with a sudden realization. "I thought he was sounding the alarm because of the taxi. But he must have been warning me about that Imp."

"You have a Willaweeper?"

"He's in my braid."

"I was wondering about the braids."

"I know. They're not great."

"I like them." He smiled, revealing teeth that looked as though they had been painstakingly chiseled out of white abalone shells. He reached over and gave the braids a jiggle. "They look good on you."

This made me blush like crazy. I'm really good at

controlling my expression—a perk of all those years playing with chess hustlers—but right now my face was calling the shots.

I suddenly felt a hard shove against my chest and I fell back, catching myself before my spine hit the ground.

"Katerina!" Tom cried, jumping to his feet. I turned around to see the small scrap of radiance behind me, its edges quivering as though it were laughing.

"If you don't behave, I'll feed you to a Sea Withen!" Tom's expression, usually so lighthearted, turned fearsome. He fixed his blue eyes on the glowing form, which grew still under his gaze. After a moment, Tom turned to me and winked.

"What is that thing?" I asked.

"Not a thing! Shh, you'll hurt her feelings. Come on." He walked backward and gestured for me to follow him. "They're almost ready."

"What are?"

"You'll see!"

14

THE ATTACK

"Are other Imps here?" I asked as we made our way up the rocky bank.

"No. Imps never live with other Imps. They're out there." He nodded toward the sea, but when I stared into the fog, he added, "You won't see them. This is the Vapour Archipelago. The fog never lifts."

"Never?"

"Never ever."

At the top of the bank, the land flattened out and thin grasses grew in tufted clumps out of fractures in the rocky ground. Now I could see that we were on a small island, not much more than a giant rock bursting out of the sea. It was the sort of island that you might sail past and think, "That would be a good spot for a picnic or a quick pee."

"Do you live here all alone?" I asked him. I hadn't meant it to sound like I felt sorry for him, but I knew it did.

"Of course not!" he said indignantly.

"Well . . . who else lives here?"

"Them." He pointed to what I had thought were rock

formations. Now I saw they weren't rocks at all. Instead, they appeared to be giant beehives. There were three of them, all nearly as tall as I was, and spun from some sort of fine gray filament.

"Just how big are the bees on this island?" I asked.

"Not bees, Nell. Ghosts."

"Ghosts?" I squinted at the hives. "What, like actual ghosts?"

"Of course."

"Is that what Katerina is? A ghost?"

A flash of dusty light circled my head—Katerina announcing her presence.

"She's one of them," Tom replied.

It occurred to me that Jordan would have been beside himself to be this close to an actual ghost, and I had a stab of worry thinking about what might have happened to him in that store.

A bubble of light oozed out of a hole in the nearest hive, then ducked back inside again. Tom smiled at it fondly. "That's Abiba. The other one is Samuel. He's shy, but he's watching you."

Well, that gave me the shivery Petes, I can tell you.

"Just pretend you don't notice them, and they'll follow us."

"Why would I want them to do that?"

Tom just laughed.

He was right, though. As we walked toward a stretch of dune, my side-eyed glances caught the scudding shapes creeping behind us. The back of my neck, exposed by my braids, felt weirdly vulnerable and I hurried to stay beside Tom.

"Why are they here? The ghosts?"

"I brought them here," Tom said.

"Why would you bring ghosts here?"

Tom hesitated.

"They weren't ghosts when I brought them here," he said finally, glancing at me apprehensively to see how I would take this.

"Oh." I felt an icy grip of understanding and stopped walking.

Right.

Imps had a bad habit of taking kids, just for the fun of it, and then growing bored and forgetting about them.

"Nell, that was a long, long time ago. I don't do that anymore."

"How long ago could it have been?"

"I'm older than I look," he said.

"How much older?"

He knit his brows, then placed his hands on his hips and looked down at the ground. When he looked back up, his expression had softened. He grinned. "I'm as old as my eyes and older than my teeth."

"That's not an answer."

Tom tipped his Viking hat back on his head suddenly and gazed up at the sky. Above us, the clouds were moving quickly. It was like those time-lapsed films of storms coming in, except these clouds were perfectly white and the sky was a tropical blue. Then, without warning, Tom cried, "Race you!" and took off at a sprint. I ran too, but Katerina outpaced me—an unnerving blob of light that rushed past me, then turned and dove at me when I got too close to Tom.

It was only a matter of moments before we came to a small beach with sand so pale it looked like snow. Here and there waist-high grasses sprouted out of the sand, spiky tufts that waved in the breeze. The thick fog hovered over the ocean, so that you could only see a few feet out. Anything beyond that was hidden behind the curtain of smoky gray mist.

Tom had stopped in front of a mound of sand, legs splayed. Katerina curled herself around Tom's shoulders like a protective cat. The wind had picked up, and when I squinted I thought I could make out luminescent tendrils of Katerina's hair twisting in the breeze. There was something about the sight of them standing like that together that both mesmerized me and filled me with jealousy. Ridiculous, I know, to be jealous of a ghost, but there you have it. I'm an idiot sometimes.

Suddenly the mound of sand shivered and I saw what looked to be a very tiny hand emerge from it. The hand was no larger than a Scrabble tile and was bluish green and damp looking. With jerky movements it reached for the air, its minuscule webbed fingers twitching. A moment later its other hand pushed out of the sand, and then a damp, hairless blue-green head appeared. It was a human-ish head, but it was also something entirely else. Its large black eyes, which shifted around blindly, had no whites to them. Its nose was nothing more than a slightly raised triangle of flesh, flattening as it neared the nostrils, like a lion's snout. Its lips, though, were disturbingly human and they opened for a moment as if to say something. No words came out, but I could see its tiny, pin-sharp teeth and a thin black tongue, which emerged and swiped at the air as though tasting it. With a sudden, spasmodic movement it pulled the rest of its body out of the sand. Altogether, the creature was no longer than my hand, but it had a muscular, fully-formed body, like a miniature grown man. Well, a man with a dorsal fin running down its spine. The next second, another hand pushed through the hill of sand, and out came a creature just like the first. Then another and another.

"Finfolk," Tom said to me, grinning.

Finfolk! I had seen one of them once in the Nigh, rising out of the river at night. It had been too dark to make it out well, but the creature had definitely been much larger than these guys.

Tom knelt down and scooped one up in his hand. The little Finfolk stretched itself out in his palm, belly down. It tipped its head back and swiveled it around, like a lizard.

"They just hatched," Tom said. "The mother buries the eggs in the sand. Look, they're trying to get to the sea. They're born blind, but they know which way to go."

The baby Finfolk, dozens and dozens of them, were crawling toward the water commando style, bellies dragging against the ground, making small squeaking noises as they went. It was hard to imagine that these toylike little things with the delicate fin down their spine would grow into fearsome sea monsters. I imagined that those kitten teeth of theirs would one day become a nasty set of chompers.

The two ghosts, Samuel and Abiba, shimmered close to the ground. The edges of their bodies shifted and reshaped, but I thought I could detect their general outlines: two children lying on their bellies in the sand, watching the crawling Finfolk.

Tom took the little Finfolk over to the shore and gently placed it on a receding wave. Its long blue-green limbs began to paddle, losing its herky-jerky land movements.

The sky overhead darkened suddenly and when I looked up, I saw that the clouds had gathered directly above us. They were low in the sky, so low that they were partially obscured by the fog. I glanced over at Tom, who was staring at them fixedly, and when I looked back up, I realized that they weren't clouds at all. They were birds, large and iceberg white, with wingspans as long as a minivan. They clustered together so tightly that their wings blocked out the sky, forming a downy canopy over our heads. Except for the thunderous *whoosh* of their wings, they were utterly silent, which somehow was the most menacing thing about them. Well, right up until I saw their heads clearly. Round, owlish faces with large black eyes and beaks as thick as a pony's hoof.

One of the birds dove out of the sky, breaking ranks with the others, and scooped up a baby Finfolk in its talons.

Tom grabbed a length of driftwood off the ground and swung at the bird. He made contact and the bird tumbled to the side and dropped the tiny Finfolk back in the sand. As if on cue, the other birds swooped down, descending on the Finfolk hatchlings, making grabs for them as the babies frantically crawled toward the sea.

Tom yelled a bloody war cry and ran into the fray, swinging the driftwood like a bat. They scattered to avoid his strikes, but they quickly rebounded and dove at the tiny hatchlings again. The ghosts joined the battle too, figures of dust-speckled light that launched themselves at the birds to little effect.

I ran at the birds too, waving my arms and screaming, but that didn't stop them. One of the birds dove right in front of me, snatched up a Finfolk in its talons, and flew off with it. The sight of that poor little thing, blind and squealing as its tiny limbs frantically felt for the ground, cracked my heart in two. Tom's also, it seemed, since he let out a cry of anguish and renewed his assault on the birds with even more energy.

Then I remembered that this was the Nigh, where the Oomphalos was far more powerful than it was back home. Not only that, the Oomphalos was everywhere! I had been able to perform my best magic here.

I pulled the chopsticks out of my jacket and ran through the spells that I knew well. It was a short list, and they were nearly all animation spells.

I looked around for something to animate. There wasn't much. Sand, water, fog—natural elements that Mr. Boot had once told us were very difficult to animate, even if I did know the specific spells. Which I did not.

But there *was* the one spell that had appeared in my manual the week before. It wasn't an animation spell. In fact, I wasn't exactly sure what kind of spell it was. Its description was vague and brief: *The Miten-Ei Spell serves as an interrupter.*

I had practiced it in my room several times and hadn't noticed anything happening, but to be fair, I didn't know what I was looking for.

I held up my hands, wrists pressed together, and began the spell. The handbook had made a point of stressing that you had to keep your focus on your subject, so I fixed my mind on those birds. Instantly I felt the Oomphalos respond to my movements, as though my hands were gathering the energy that was already in the air.

Performing magic was a struggle for me in general. I couldn't "feel" my way through the spells like Crud and Annika could. Unlike their magic, mine was awkward and bumbling. But now, as my hands worked the spell, each movement seemed to contain information in some ancient silent language, a language I didn't understand but was somehow fluent in.

Although the Finfolk hatchlings couldn't see, they must have been able to sense that they were in terrible danger. They were frantic now, crawling toward the water faster and faster. As I came to the tail end of the spell, one of the birds dove down in front of me, its thick cankerous feet with their black talons stretched out toward a hatchling that had lagged behind the others. I fought the impulse to stop the spell in order to swat at the bird, but I forced myself to continue until I finished.

The spell worked swiftly and dramatically. An interrupting spell. Well, that definitely was an accurate description. There was a blinding flash of light. The thunderous sound of wings stopped on a dime. The birds hung in the air, frozen. They reminded me of the animal dioramas at the Museum of Natural History, in which stuffed vultures were posed in the middle of a hunt. The birds' white wings shadowed the ground as they hovered in the air above us, motionless. The beach grew quiet once more, except for the sound of fog-shrouded waves breaking against the shore and the squeals of the hatchlings as they continued their urgent crawl toward the sea.

15

MITEN-EI SPELL

"How did you do that?" Tom dropped the piece of driftwood and gazed up, face damp with sweat, at the petrified birds.

"Miten-Ei Spell," I whispered back. I don't know why we whispered. Maybe because it felt like the spell could be broken at any moment.

"Nice." Tom's blue eyes gazed at me with such admiration that I felt my face heat up with pride.

He looked back up at the birds and laughed, an open, wild sound of joy.

"Serves you all right, you ugly oversized chickens!" He jumped up and flicked the beak of one of the birds. There was a crackling sound and the bird's entire body crumbled into tiny white flakes that drifted to the ground, the way a burnt piece of paper disintegrates at a touch. A second later, the crackling sound came again, and the other birds crumbled as well, their ashes forming snowy white mounds on the pale sand.

Whenever you perform magic, there is this little

internal buzz you get. Maybe it's the feeling of power, I don't know. But this? This terrified me. I had destroyed those birds. All of them. Apart from the occasional spider, I'd never killed anything in my life.

I heard Tom pull in a shocked gasp of air. For a moment we both stared at the ashes littering the beach. I caught the undulating outline of Katerina's hand grabbing Tom's, like a kid needing comfort. Samuel and Abiba circled the beach, their filmy, light-filled bodies stirring up a breeze that swept the ashes into the ocean. A burial of sorts.

"I've never seen anything like that before," Tom said. His voice was solemn as he stared at me.

"I didn't want to kill them," I said. "I didn't know—"

It was then that the light on the beach changed. The heavy fog lifted like a snapped window shade. The sea spread out before us, suddenly visible, glassy green blue, dotted with other small islands as far as I could see.

Back when I was in third grade my father wanted me to try out for the school play. They were doing *The Wizard of Oz*. He thought it would help me overcome my shyness, except I was never actually shy. I just don't love being the center of attention. Anyway, I must have tanked my audition because the teacher decided I'd be better off as stage crew, which suited me just fine. Except during the opening night performance, while I swept "witch water" confetti off the darkened stage between scenes, the kid in the lighting booth pushed the wrong button. The whole stage was suddenly flooded with light. I couldn't see the audience but they could see me. I froze, horrified by the thought of all those eyes on me. I just stood there until someone had to run on stage and pull me off.

That's how it felt now.

Like I was exposed when I shouldn't be. Like something was watching me with intense curiosity.

On the other islands, I could see lone figures pacing the banks of the now fogless ocean. Imps, I guessed. A boat similar to Tom's appeared from behind one of the islands, moving toward us with surprising speed. Its single rectangular sail, a faded red color, was cupped as it collected the wind.

"Duck down behind the grass," Tom said, "and stay very still."

I crouched down behind a clump of tall grass, panic beginning to rise in my chest.

"What's happening?" I whispered.

Tom didn't answer, but he signaled to Katerina, Abiba, and Samuel, and they gathered close to me. Between the stems of grass and the luminescent bodies of the ghosts, I caught glimpses of the boat and the Imp inside it who was rowing. Dark haired and long limbed, he rowed with graceful, effortless movements, the water barely riffling around his oars as they cut through the water. When he came close, the Imp stood. "Heyo, Tom!"

"Heyo, Lysander!" Tom called back, less enthusiastically.

"What's happened to the fog?"

"How should I know?" Tom crossed his arms over his chest.

Lysander was quiet for a moment, studying Tom's island while keeping perfect balance as his boat rocked gently in the waves. His eyes landed on the ghosts in front of me and he flashed a smile so brilliant and disturbing it stopped my breath for a moment. An Imp smile.

Abiba seemed to grow taller, the edges of her diaphanous body spreading like a threat, while I willed myself to stay perfectly still.

"I see you're still hanging on to your little kiddies," Lysander said.

Tom made no reply.

"I don't understand the point of that, personally," Lysander continued. "What use are they? They're all raggedy. No fun at all, and frankly they give me the creeps when they fade away like that. I'll tell you what I'll do to help you out, Tom. I'll put them in a sack, tie it up tight." He mimed tying a knot and pulling it tight. "And I'll toss them in the ocean. It's what I did with my own kiddies. What do you say, Tom?"

I felt the ghosts around me bristle, their lights flickering quickly.

"What do I say?" Tom's voice was cold with rage. "I say that you are a cowardly flap-mouthed pig of an Imp!"

This seemed to knock the bluster out of Lysander. I could see his balance shift, making his boat teeter. He recovered himself quickly, though, and shot back, "Me cowardly? Ha! Which one of us worked for the Magicians?" After he said the word "Magicians," he spit into the ocean with disgust.

"Only once," Tom responded. "And not for long."

"Oi, kiddies!" Lysander addressed this to the ghosts. "Do you know how Magicians pay Imps for their services? They give them a Human child. A living Human child."

The three ghosts were still, listening.

"Now, kiddies, let's everyone guess what Tom will do when he gets his Human child." Lysander waved his hand in the air, like a kid in a classroom. "Me! Me! I go first. My guess is that he will forget all about you. He'll only care about his new living friend. You kiddies might disappear, phhht, and he'd never even notice—"

"Not true!" Tom cried.

"True!" Lysander called back. He nimbly shifted his weight as an errant wave lifted and rocked his boat. "Your turn, kiddies," he said to the ghosts. "What's your guess? What will Tom do when he gets his real live Human?"

There was a pause and Katerina produced a shiver of dusty light, like a dog shaking off water. Her luminous body rose and twisted, then hooked itself around the tall grass in front of me.

"Katerina!" Tom growled before he sprang at her, but he couldn't stop her in time.

Katerina bent the grass to one side, putting me in full view of the Imp.

When the Imp saw me, his eyes widened. "What's this I see? She looks very fresh."

"*Wickle-wickle-feee! Wickle-wickle-feee!*" I heard Winston calling from my right braid.

It was a little late for a warning.

In fact, Lysander was already rowing straight for the island with tremendous speed.

"Don't come any closer, Lysander!" Tom picked up a large rock and hurled it at the boat. It missed by a hairsbreadth, which made me wonder if Tom had meant it as a warning. Lysander stopped rowing for a moment. But only a moment. His oars sliced at the water again until he was so close he could have hopped out of his boat and waded ashore.

"*Wickle-wickle-feee! Wickle-wickle-feee!*"

Winston was screeching in my ear now. I don't know what prompted me to look up at the sky. It was clear and cloudless, yet something had caught my eye. There was a black dot in the far distance, just above the horizon. Its movements were too awkward to be a bird. I thought it might be an air balloon being buffeted around by the wind, but Winston's insistent screeching made me wonder if it was something more sinister.

Standing in his boat, gazing up at the sky behind him, Lysander had spotted it too.

"Magician," he said.

16

Lysander's Faering

I felt my chest tighten with fear so raw that for a moment no words would come out of my mouth.

"Is it a Magician?" I asked Tom, who was now staring up at the moving speck in the sky.

"I think so."

"They're coming for me," I said. It was a statement that Tom didn't bother denying.

"Get in my faering," Lysander said, pointing to his boat.

"I'll take my own," Tom replied.

"My girl is blazing fast and she can sniff out the wind. By the time you get your piece of junk in the water, the Magician will be here."

I hated to admit it, but Lysander was right.

"We'll go with him," I said to Tom.

"You go. I can't."

"Why?"

"He won't let the ghosts in the boat." His eyes cut over to the ghosts, who were standing together, watching us.

"And if that Magician is coming to search the island, I'm not leaving them alone here."

I turned back to Lysander. "The ghosts are coming too."

"No ghosts," Lysander countered firmly. "Ghosts in a boat bring bad luck."

We were at a stalemate. Tom wouldn't leave his ghosts and I wouldn't leave Tom and the little black dot in the sky was getting larger and larger by the second.

Playing chess in Washington Square Park had gotten me into dumpster-sized trouble over the years. In fact, you could argue that chess had caused this whole predicament in the first place, since River had been whisked away to the Nigh while I was playing my first game with the chess hustlers. But chess had also taught me that there was almost always a way out of a tight spot.

"I can protect the boat," I announced to Lysander. I took out my chopsticks and felt the Oomphalos instantly collect around the sticks.

Tom understood and backed me up. "She can, Lysander. She's a magician, a powerful one. She's with the AOA. She's the one who made the fog vanish."

Accidentally, but never mind.

Lysander's eyes grew wide. The Imp was clearly impressed. "All right."

I began the Frishin Spell. It was a pretty dumb spell. It made old things look brand new again, but only very temporarily. I had tried it on my favorite pair of old jeans, which I'd ruined with some bleach. It made the splotchy white marks disappear immediately. The jeans stiffened and turned spanking-new blue. But a moment later they returned to their stained and shabby old selves.

When I finished the Frishin Spell, the wood on Lysander's boat gleamed a pale gold, untouched by weather, and his sail was as crisp as an ironed sheet, its faded red now bright deep vermillion. It only lasted for the blink of an eye, but it did the trick.

"There," I said, "it's under a protection spell."

Lysander was suitably impressed.

"Okay," he said "The ghosts can come."

"Take Samuel," Tom said to me, as Katerina wrapped herself around Tom's neck, while he carried the other ghost—Abiba presumably—in his arms.

"What?"

"They can't touch water," he explained as he waded into the shallows, heading for the faering. "If too much water gets on them, it . . ." He glanced quickly at Abiba and lowered his voice. "We'll just have to be really careful, okay?"

I nodded and turned to Samuel, who was shimmering beside me, waiting. I reached out and awkwardly picked him up, not quite knowing how you were supposed to hold a ghost. I felt him settle into my arms, a bundle of weight-less warmth. I waded through the water, handing Samuel off to Tom, who was already on the boat, then climbing in myself.

Lysander had been right about his boat. The faering *was*

blazing fast as it headed out into the open sea. It seemed to just barely skim the waves as Lysander rowed with ferocious strength. I'd forgotten how strong Imps were. They just looked like slender boys, but I had once experienced Tom's iron grip, and let me tell you that boy could have taken down Crud in an arm wrestling match every time.

Up in the sky, the Magician was no longer a distant dot. Now I could see her clearly. A woman dressed in drab clothes, like an office worker. She flew in a peculiar upright way that reminded me of angels in paintings. But this was no angel.

"Can we outrun her?" I asked Lysander.

"Of course we can." His answer was bold and cocky, but I could see that Tom wasn't so sure. His pale hair was whipping in the wind as he kept an anxious eye on the sky. The ghosts were huddled together in the stern of the boat, their light stained a sickly dappled gray where the sea spray had hit them, as though the water had extinguished their light at the places where it touched.

We skirted around other islands. I sometimes caught a glimpse of a lone boy, another Imp, watching us as we flew past. Here and there, towering out of the water, were enormous stone structures, lumpy and monstrous. They seemed to cluster around each other, like a gathering of giants.

Just as Lysander had said, the faering seemed to find the wind, shifting like a dog on a scent. Nevertheless, the Magician was gaining on us. I could make out the glint of a silver buckle at her waist and the pointed toes of her shoes.

Her arms were lifted as she flew, her hands twisting subtly.

The wind, which had been coming from behind us, now changed. It was pushing back against us. I felt it press against my cheek and hiss in my left ear. The boat responded by listing to the right and slowing down.

"Ready!" Lysander called to Tom, who sprang up and stood by the sail.

"Ready!"

Tom maneuvered the sail. The faering instantly picked up speed and Lysander matched it with ever more powerful rowing. But after a few minutes, the wind whipped around and forced the little faering to the right again. The boat stalled, as though it were uncertain what was wanted of it.

I looked up and saw the Magician only yards away, her slender hands moving in what was undoubtably a spell.

"She's changing the wind!" I yelled.

Tom and Lysander looked up at her just as the Magician swept both hands downward. All around us the sea began to thrash as the wind seemed to come from everywhere at once. I lurched over toward the ghosts and tried to use my body to block the water from them as the faering rocked helplessly. The waves seemed to be fighting the spell, their frothy peaks punching upward. A wave rose up along the side and caught Abiba, whose light sizzled and sparked against its touch. She shrieked, a thin, distant sound, and then the faering's bow plunged down sharply and we all fell forward. Just when it seemed we were destined to be tossed into the sea, the boat righted itself.

"Watch out, up ahead!" Lysander called.

"I see it!" Tom called back as he worked the sail.

It took me a moment to blink the spray out of my eyes before I spotted what they were looking at: a group of those towering stones, dead ahead.

"Row!" Tom called to Lysander.

"I'm trying!" he said, clearly struggling to control the boat.

Looking up, I could see the Magician was lower in the sky and her hands were busy. She was directing the wind and the current, herding us straight for the huge monoliths.

"Nell!" Tom called to me. "She's going to send us into the rocks."

I nodded and we locked eyes. I knew what he was thinking. I had thought of it too.

The Miten-Ei Spell. It would stop her the way it had stopped those birds. It would also kill her.

I wrapped my hands around my chopsticks. My entire body was shaking, but whether it was from fear of those monstrous rocks or dread at what I was about to do, I didn't know. I lifted my chopsticks, bracing my left hand against the side of the boat as we were propelled forward by the relentless wind.

I looked up at the Magician. She seemed to be struggling to stay upright in the gale of her own making, her body tossed this way and that. She rose and fell, her dark hair whipping around like seaweed in waves. She didn't look like Folk—I knew from last time I was in the Nigh that Magicians seemed to be a different species from Folk. In fact, Magicians looked very much like regular people from back home. At that moment the Magician glanced down at me. Our eyes met, and the enormity of what I was about to do, to take someone's life from them, made me freeze.

"Nell?" Tom called out to me.

"I . . . I can't!" I called back.

He fixed his sea-blue eyes on me for a moment. Then he nodded and let go of the sail.

17

ʘSLAND OF ꟻOAM

"**W**hat are you doing?" Lysander yelled.

But Tom knew what I knew. That it was hopeless. That this Magician would do what she wanted. She was too strong for us, and I wouldn't kill her, couldn't kill her, so there we were.

The Magician seemed to understand that we were no longer fighting her. She drifted lower and lower, like a balloon losing its air. The wind settled. The boat rocked gently now in the becalmed water.

Lysander began to row. The little faering, released from the grip of the Magician's winds, responded instantly.

"Over there!" Lysander called to Tom, pointing to a small island of white beach sand just ahead. Tom began to work the sail again so that we were now charging for the island, although I couldn't see the point of it. Never mind that the island was barely large enough for three people to stand on; it would simply make us sitting ducks for the Magician.

I looked back at the Magician, who, seeing that we had

used the lull in her spell to slip out of her grasp, began to work her spell once more.

The wind was picking up again, soft at first but gaining strength by the second. Not only that, but overhead, in the distance, an ominous purple-black cloud slithered across the sky, zigzagging like a snake. This was magic. No cloud had ever looked like that, pulling bits of white cumulous clouds into itself as it twisted along, absorbing them into its blackness, growing larger by the second.

"Tom!" I pointed up. His face turned grim when he saw the cloud, and his eyes darted over toward Katerina, Samuel, and Abiba.

The ghosts! What would happen to them if that cloud broke open and there was a downpour? There was nowhere for them to take cover in this open boat.

The ghosts must have seen the cloud too, because Katerina darted over to Tom and clutched his waist. She was just a scared little girl really, and my heart tightened with panic. Samuel and Abiba stayed where they were. I thought I could make out glimpses of their anxious faces appearing and disappearing within the glow of light.

The little island was dead ahead now. Yet as we came close, I realized it wasn't an island at all. It was a patch of white foam formed by fine bubbles that floated on the ocean's surface. Once we pulled alongside, Tom put up a hand and Lysander stopped rowing.

The sky was growing darker by the second. In the distance I could see a gray column of rain pouring out of the black cloud as it slithered its way closer and closer.

The Magician had dropped in altitude and was hovering only yards above us. She looked young and quick and dangerous.

"Stop the cloud!" I yelled up to her.

"Give me a good reason to."

"I'll go with you. Stop the cloud and I'll go with you."

The Magician laughed. "You'll go with me anyway," she replied. Her voice was liquid smooth and calm. She sounded like a nurse telling her patient that the needle was only going to hurt for a minute.

"I won't! Not unless you stop the cloud!" I yelled back.

Lysander shot up suddenly, one oar still in hand. He leapt at me, grabbing my arm and twisting it so that I had to stand up. "Just take her and let it rain!" he said to the Magician. "She's more trouble than she's worth anyway, and I don't need my faering smashed to bits for her sake."

Of course, I thought bitterly. Of course, he'd betray us! I should never have insisted we go with him. Now Tom's ghosts would drown, and I would be taken, and it was all for nothing.

A look of surprise, then satisfaction, passed across the Magician's face.

"What a clever little Imp you are," the Magician said. She swooped down awkwardly beside the boat until her pointed shoes touched the waves, and she reached out to take me from Lysander's grip. Lysander yanked me backward a second before she could grab me, and something burst out of the foamy water. At first, I thought it was a man in a scuba diving suit. Its head and body were smoothly glistening, as if it were covered in blackish-green neoprene. But then I saw the large black eyes with no whites to them. The flat, triangular nose. And the dorsal fin running down its back.

Finfolk. And not a baby Finfolk either. This one was easily as big as Crud, maybe bigger.

The Magician shrieked as the Finfolk flung one arm around her neck. She struggled in its grasp, but a second later the Finfolk pulled her beneath the water. We waited, breathless, watching the roiling white foam all around the boat. The foam fizzed and churned, then bubbled up as though the water were boiling. After a few moments, the bubbles dissolved. The foam dispersed and vanished. Overhead the sky grew light again.

"Is she gone?" I whispered.

Lysander nodded.

Tom smiled, grabbing Lysander by the shoulders and shaking him. "What a clever little Imp you are, Lysander!" He mimicked the Magician's words.

Abiba rose, her light glowing brightly now. She went up to Lysander and stretched out one glowing hand toward him.

"What does it want from me?" Lysander asked, leaning away from her uneasily.

"Her name is Abiba," Tom answered, "and she wants to thank you."

Lysander glanced down at Abiba's hand. He took it tentatively, watching as it pulsed pale rose light against his own hand before she took it away again. A ghost's handshake. It seemed to embarrass Lysander. His cheeks had turned ruddy and he shrugged one shoulder.

"I told you I didn't like Magicians," he said.

"How did you know the Finfolk was here?" I asked.

"Foam," Tom and Lysander said together. Tom added, "When you see the foam, there's always a pod of Finfolk below."

"Finfolk don't like Magicians either," Lysander said.

Tom gazed back toward the Vapour Archipelago, at the smattering of small islands dotting the turquoise water.

"We can't go back there." Tom's voice was grim. "They'll send other Magicians."

"I can't go home. I've failed the trials," I said. "They'll perform the Umglick Spell on me. This is it. This is my only chance to help River. I can't wait any longer."

We looked at each other and Tom's expression brightened, changing on a dime, like it sometimes did.

"My home and your home. Those are the two places we can't go back to. Which leaves everywhere else." He placed his hands on his hips, chin lifted, and said to Lysander, "I need to fetch my faering."

"No you don't. We're taking this one," Lysander replied.

"We're? We're? Since when are you going?"

Lysander nodded toward the ghosts. "Do you want them to drown in your little floating frying pan?"

Lysander's attitude toward the ghosts seemed to have taken a 180, but Tom didn't notice as he rose to the insult.

"My faering is legions better than your piece of old driftwood!"

Just as the two of them seemed ready to pounce on each other, an idea popped into my head.

"His faering is fast, Tom," I said. In all honesty, Tom's faering looked a little long in the tooth, as my dad liked to say.

"And she put a spell on it," Lysander reminded Tom.

"Right, I did," I said. "Remember, Tom?"

Tom muttered something under his breath.

"Good, that's settled," I said. "And I know where we should go."

18

MERMAIDS AND SASQUATCHES

Without a Magician casting spells on the wind, Lysander's faering raced through the water with ease. In fact, the wind was so obliging that Lysander no longer needed to row. While Tom worked the sail, with Katerina by his side, Lysander sat back, legs outstretched. He fixed his attention on me, his eyes locking squarely on mine, like a gun-sight finding its target. He smiled.

"It won't work," I said.

His smile wilted slightly with confusion. "What won't?"

"I don't beguile," I said.

From his position by the sail, Tom laughed. "She's immune to Imps."

I wasn't entirely sure that was true, but I could at least detect when Imps were working their particular kind of charm.

Lysander gave me a searching look, then let out a small huff. "Well, that's boring."

He stood up and moved to sit beside Samuel and Abiba. "You two like me anyway, don't you?" he asked. It was said in such a sad, lonely sort of way. I thought of all those Imps, living by themselves on their islands, cut off even from each other by the fog. Well, until recently anyway. Abiba looped her gossamer arm through Lysander's, and Samuel moved closer to him.

The sea stretched out endlessly in all directions. Every so often, there would be a spit of land in the far distance, but that was all. Once a boulder, huge and domed, rose out of the waves, then sank back again.

"Whale," Tom said when he saw me watching it with furrowed brows.

"Whale? Like a regular whale? Are yours like the ones we have?"

"Ha!" Lysander blurted out, a bitter laugh that was whisked out to sea in the breeze. "Some magician! She doesn't even know that the Nigh came before the Hither!"

"She knows!" Tom shot back at Lysander.

It was true, I had heard that before. That we had all lived in the Nigh to begin with.

"Where do you think all your animals come from?" Lysander pressed me. "All your plants and your fish and your everything. From the Nigh."

"We don't have things like Finfolk in the Hither," I countered.

"Oh no? What do you think mermaids are?" he said.

"I think they're nonsense."

"He's right, Nell," Tom said. "Look, you've gotten in and out of the Nigh through Wickets. Well, other creatures travel through them too, sometimes by accident, sometimes just out of curiosity. And every so often people in the Hither will spot one of these creatures and think they saw a mermaid or a Sasquatch—"

"Wait, you have Sasquatches here?"

"Grubbles," Tom and Lysander said in unison.

"They're pretty common," Tom said. "Folk can't stand them, because they dig up gardens and they smell like garbage. A lot of Folk would probably love to send them all over to the Hither if they could."

We sailed on and on, time melting as we raced across on the unbroken expanse of sea. The sky overhead darkened and night fell. I reached into the chest pocket of my jacket and pulled out the little scrap of paper with the cryptic scrawl.

THERE MAY BE A WAY TO BRING HIM HOME.
THE GOLDEN IMAGINARIUM.

I read it over a few times, then refolded it carefully and put it back in my pocket.

It had been a long day. Exhaustion swept over me, and I rested my head in my hands. My eyes grew heavy and I shut them—I'll just close them for a moment, I thought—but when I woke up, the sky was the color of baby clothes, pale pinks and blues. I'd slept through the night.

In the distance, the familiar skyline emerged out of the

haze, like a row of house keys standing on end. New York City. For a moment, I forgot that I was in the Nigh, and I felt a rush of excitement to be home again . . . until Samuel drifted past me toward the bow of the boat to see better, shedding flecks of light in the breeze.

"Good morning," Tom said, seeing me lift my head. He was still at the sail, looking perfectly fresh.

"We thought you were never going to wake up," said Lysander, who was now rowing again.

"Oh no! My dad!" I cried out. "He's going to be out of his mind with worry!"

"Mr. Boot and Vanessa will sort it out," Tom reassured me.

"That worries me," I said.

The river narrowed, herded between the City and the land mass across from it—Staten Island, in my world. But here, in the Nigh, it was simply a stretch of forest with towering trees, a wide swath of which were leaning drunkenly against one another, where a bad storm must have passed through.

As we traveled farther north, the river grew more congested with ships, big slow-moving things with tall and complicated masts. There were smaller boats too, all with sails, but none moved as quickly as Lysander's facring.

"Put your hood up," Tom told me, as we approached one of the large ships, "and slump down."

I flipped my hood over my head and ducked my head down, crossing my arms over my knees, while still able to peek out. On the deck of the ship, crews of men worked great lengths of rope as they unfurled masts.

"Weigh anchor!" I heard someone call, and watched as several men pushed a large wooden wheel, like donkeys attached to a mill. A tremendous iron chain rose up from the depths of the water, an anchor attached to the end.

The men were Folk. You could always tell Folk. Though these men had skin that was sun-roughened and their hair was greasy, they still managed to radiate that odd Folk glimmer that caught your eye and kept it.

A few of the men watched our faering slip past, gazing at us with unfriendly faces.

Lysander stood in the boat, raised both arms in the air, and shouted up at them, "That's right, boys! Get an eyeful of glorious us!"

"Lysander, shhht!" Tom growled at him.

One of the men in the ship leaned over the railing and spat at us. It missed by yards but he made his point.

"What's their problem?" I asked Tom.

Tom shrugged. "Imps have never been too popular with Folk."

Still standing, Lysander turned his back to the ship and began to undo his pants, apparently intending on mooning them, but Tom grabbed his shirt and yanked him back down in his seat.

Up ahead, in the distance, rising out of a small island in the river, was a statue of an old man in a hospital gown with wildly disheveled hair. One hand was raised in the air, holding a television remote control. The Statue of Liberty. That was the Nigh to a tee: just like home, right up until it wasn't.

19

PIDDLEBANK

We soon arrived in Piddlebank, a small village spliced by a winding canal. The canal was so narrow that the faering had to move over to let a family of ducks swim by. I had been in Piddlebank before. Back then I was told it was a part of Brooklyn, but you could have fooled me. Instead of clothing boutiques and coffee shops, the banks of the canal were lined with small cottages, some cobbled up with lumpy stone and others that looked like they'd been slapped together with mud, then whitewashed. Their roofs were made of some thick, brown shaggy stuff, as if a giant bear had fallen asleep on top of the house. But though the houses were rough and ready, nearly all them were freshened up with flower boxes and brightly painted shutters. Some had little orchards beside them or tidy vegetable gardens.

The last time I'd been in Piddlebank it was the middle of the night, and a moonless night at that. In the light of day, I saw just how pretty the place was. Billowy green farmland, much of it ribboned with crops, stretched out behind the houses on both sides of the canal. Grazing in the fields, like roaming chess pieces, were black goats and white sheep. The place was quiet too. Even the air was quiet, without a puff of breeze.

Tom sat across from me as we drifted through the canal, listening to the rhythmic hiss of Lysander's oars cutting through the water and the occasional distant bleats of a sheep.

"It feels like nothing bad could happen in this place, doesn't it?" I said dreamily.

"Is that why you wanted to come here?" Tom asked.

His question pulled me up short. "Of course not. I wanted to come to Piddlebank because I think there's someone here who can help us."

Still, there was a little knot of truth to Tom's question, and that thought nagged at me. I wondered if I'd made the wrong decision coming to Piddlebank. I'd been driven here by a hunch, and maybe that hunch was wrong. Or worse, maybe I'd fooled myself altogether just because I had once felt safe here, and cared for.

"Which house is it?" Tom asked.

"I'm not sure. It was so dark when I was here last time, I really didn't see it well. I know it was past a bridge. . . ."

The problem was there were many bridges spanning the canal. We'd been beneath two already and there was another just ahead.

The sound of hammering, and its heckling echo, broke the silence. A woman was standing in front of her house by the canal bank, pounding a wooden post into the ground, where a half dozen planks of wood formed a partially finished fence around a garden. When she saw us, she stopped hammering on the spot and her eyes grew wide.

"Imps?! Imps in Piddlebank? What's next?"

"Ghosts too, lady." Lysander jabbed a thumb at Katerina, Abiba, and Samuel, smiling. "What do you think of that?"

"Imps and ghosts, Mams!" This joyous outburst came from a boy who had peered out at us from behind the partially finished fence.

"Has everything turned on its head? Go away!" the woman shouted at us. "We don't want any part of you here! Go! Go!" She held up her hammer like she might fling it at us, so I threw back my hood. The sight of a Human made her pause, the hammer still gripped in her raised hand.

"We're looking for Mrs. Nerriberry," I said. "Can you tell us what house she's in?"

"And a Human too, Mams!" The little boy was beside himself with excitement.

"Oh, it's Mrs. Nerriberry you want, is it?" The woman's mouth twisted with disapproval. "Not a shock. She invites all sorts of disgusting creatures in her home."

"I like Mrs. Nerriberry's disgusting creatures," the boy said.

"No you don't," the woman told him.

"I do. I like them." He turned to us and said, "She lives in the third house past the next bridge."

"Look what you did!" the woman cried, and Lysander

quickly rowed off, leaving the two of them to shout at each other, the little one giving as good as he got.

We arrived at Mrs. Nerriberry's a few minutes later. Her home was a Jenga jumble of stones, so haphazardly piled that the place looked ready to topple if someone pulled the wrong one out. In the light of day, I could see that it wasn't as well kept as some of the other houses. The grass in the yard was long and weedy and was littered with various buckets and troughs. A child's rope-and-wood swing dangled high up from the branch of a tree, the rope wrapped around and around the branch.

Tom, Lysander, and I paraded up the crooked path, while the ghosts hung back, hovering warily near the tree with the swing. When we reached the front door, I lifted my hand to knock, then hesitated. I wondered if Tom and Lysander should go back to the boat so that I could introduce them slowly, but before I could suggest it, Lysander reached over my shoulder and rapped loudly on the door. It was opened by a Folk woman with a messy tangle of dark curls and a damp-faced look of impatience.

"You again?" she cried out when she saw me. "What are you thinking? I ought to deliver you straight to the Magicians and end the suspense!"

My heart sank at this greeting. But the very next moment, Mrs. Nerriberry threw her arms around me and hugged me to her. It was a mother's hug. I don't need anyone to feel sorry for me or anything, but if my own mother had ever hugged me like that, I didn't remember it. It felt so nice that I closed my eyes and didn't pull away like I usually do when people hug me. After a moment, Mrs. Nerriberry's grip loosened, and I lifted my head to see that she had finally clocked the strange little troupe behind me. With sudden and surprising force, she grabbed me by the shoulders and shoved me into her house. Picking up a tattered old umbrella from beside the door, she thrust it at Tom and Lysander with threatening jabs that made them jump backward.

"Listen to me, you wretched creatures," she said to them. "If you ever get near this child again, I will send a legion of Wormbreathers after you, and don't think I won't."

"No, no, it's okay, Mrs. Nerriberry!" I cried, reaching out to grab the umbrella. "They're friends. We all sailed here together."

Mrs. Nerriberry didn't drop the umbrella, but when she saw the ghosts hovering at the bottom of the path, she let out a little "Oooh!" in a much softer voice.

"This is Tom and Lysander," I said. "And back there are Abiba and Katerina. Samuel is . . . oh, he's hiding behind the tree."

Mrs. Nerriberry marched straight up to the ghosts, hissing to me as she passed, "What were you thinking to take these little ones in a boat? Don't you know what water does to them?" I started to defend myself, but she ignored me as she hustled us all into her home.

20

MRS. NERRIBERRY

Inside, it was a very humble sort of place. Its dirt floors had shallow divots in which small puddles had formed. Here and there, vines crept up the walls and dripped down from the ceilings. Roughly cobbled cupboards lined the tiny kitchen, and the living room was littered with children's toys and little bowls and piles of rags. Mrs. Nerriberry settled the ghosts into chairs beside a fireplace in which a low flame crackled.

"Look at that! They like the fire," Tom said with surprise, smiling at the ghosts, who were now glowing as if someone had just put fresh bulbs in them.

"Well, of course they do," Mrs. Nerriberry replied disapprovingly. "Anyone who knows a smidge about ghosts knows that they love a fire."

Tom walked up to the fireplace mantel and stroked a sleek, black catlike creature that was stretched out across it. It reacted to Tom's touch by puffing out a pair of wings, its feathers bristling.

"Hello, little cattywampus," Tom cooed.

For a moment it seemed like Mrs. Nerriberry was going to call Tom away from the creature, but the cattywampus settled its wings against its back again and made a contented humming sound.

"I found her wandering along the canal, all skin and bones. I fattened her up and now she doesn't want to leave. Like that Jiggle-Merry there." Mrs. Nerriberry pointed to a little oily-skinned creature, no bigger than a thumb, who was paddling lazily in one of the puddles in the dirt floor.

That was the thing about Mrs. Nerriberry's house. There were creatures all over it, though you didn't notice them at first because there was so much clutter around. Once you saw one of them, you began to notice the others, too. Some were clinging to the vines that ran up her walls, or hanging from curtain rods, or slithering up the side of the furniture. Mrs. Nerriberry's house was a makeshift veterinary clinic for unusual creatures.

Now I looked more closely at one of the piles of rags on the floor and saw that it was an animal. Its fur was dull and gray and it was so thin that its hips jutted out above its sunken torso. Its face was squashed in like a pug and its ears were large and pointed.

"Oh, he's a skrill!" I cried.

"She," Mrs. Nerriberry corrected me as she headed to the kitchen. "My brother Reynold brought her here just last night. He wouldn't say how he found her—the man is ridiculously secretive about the goings on in his life—but a blessing that he did because she was close to death."

"What's wrong with her?" I asked.

"She was attacked near a Wicket."

"Attacked? By who?" I asked.

"By *what*, you mean. Some awful creature, apparently. Last night, the poor dear murmured something about horns and stripes and tusks. It sounded like a thing made up of leftover bits. I know my critters backward and forward, but I never heard of anything like this one. In any case, it completely destroyed the Wicket and nearly killed her in the process. She had a terrible gash down her side— ripped her right open—thank goodness I'm handy with a needle."

Mrs. Nerriberry went into the kitchen and rummaged around, grabbing things and placing them on plates, which she carried out to the rough wood table in the main room. "Help yourselves. It's nothing fancy, but then I don't know what you Imps eat. Roots and berries?"

"I'm partial to candy," said Tom hopefully.

"No candy, but I have some nice Iced Nippers." She pointed to a plate of small flower-shaped cakes with green icing. "Go on. Nell, you too. Hoi! You in the back there." She squinted at Lysander, who'd been standing at the far end of the room, watching Mrs. Nerriberry with shy fascination. "Why are you hiding in the corner like a mouse? Come here and tuck in."

Lysander obeyed on the spot.

"Now," Mrs. Nerriberry said to me as she heaved herself into a chair at the table and set a steaming mug in front of her. "Let's hear it, Nell. Tell me why you can't seem to stay in your own world."

I told her. I didn't plan on telling her everything—just the important stuff—but it all spilled out anyway. Maybe it was because she was such a good listener. Her eyes widened at the scary parts and she gasped when I told her about what the Magicians had done when they found us the last time. When I talked about my dad, she smiled approvingly, and yeah, the thought occurred to me that if they ever met, which was highly unlikely, they would probably hit it off. When I told her about our recent run-in with the Magician at sea, Mrs. Nerriberry sat back and scrutinized Tom and Lysander. "Well, I'm not so pigheaded that I won't admit when I'm wrong. Perhaps Imps have some scruples after all."

"There are some bad Imps, to be sure," Lysander said to her, his tone surprisingly polite. "But Tom and I are different."

They were the first words he'd uttered since we'd arrived. He seemed to be on his best behavior. It occurred to me that although he might be very, very old like Tom, he was still basically a boy. A boy without a mother or father. I don't know why, but Mrs. Nerriberry felt like everyone's mother somehow. Mine included, if I'm being honest.

"But why have you come here, Nell?" Mrs. Nerriberry asked. "Not that I'm not happy to see you, I am, but I don't see how I can help you either."

"I need to find Mary Carpenter," I told her. "If anyone will know where River is, it's her."

"Mary Carpenter?" Mrs. Nerriberry looked perplexed. "I wouldn't have the slightest idea where to find Mary Carpenter."

"I know, but your brother Reynold might."

This brought Mrs. Nerriberry up short. I could see the idea playing out in her face. She seemed on the brink of dismissing it, then was struck by the possibility that there might be something to it.

"Reynold has always been very hush-hush about his travels," she said carefully, "and he *does* seem to know things that no one else does. . . ."

I nodded. "There are spies in the Nigh," I said, referring to what Vanessa had told me. "People who are working against the Magicians. I remembered things you told me about your brother last time I was here, and I thought maybe he's one of those spies. So I took a chance." I looked over at Tom and Lysander, then at the ghosts, who were watching us, listening. "We all took a chance."

"The Magicians will know you're in the Nigh now," Mrs. Nerriberry mused. "Which means they might have followed you to Piddlebank."

"There's a chance," I admitted reluctantly.

Mrs. Nerriberry nodded, her face grave.

"Look, I know that I'm putting you at risk—" I started, but Mrs. Nerriberry held up her hand to stop me.

"Piddlebank has always kept to its own ways—the old

ways—and we're proud of it. Too proud, if you ask me. It's easy to be uppity about things when we spend our time puttering around our little lives, fussing over our vegetable gardens. But we're all part of the Nigh. All of us. And if terrible things are happening in one part of the Nigh, they will come to all parts of the Nigh eventually, including Piddlebank, whether a little Human girl brings it to us now or someone else brings it later. So that's my way of saying, if I can help you, I will."

I felt Tom's hand grab mine beneath the table and hold it tight.

"Reynold can be secretive, but he's still my little brother. If he knows where Mary Carpenter is, I'll worm it out of him."

At that moment, there was a tremendous CRACK! and the front door burst open.

21

REYNOLD

A wooden barrel rolled through the door. It crashed against a wall, and a small boy flew out of it, squealing with laughter even as he scrambled to his feet. At the sight of Mrs. Nerriberry's horrified face, though, the boy stopped laughing.

"Are we in trouble, Mams?" he asked her.

"Look around, dummy," said an older girl in a mangy wool jacket, who had walked into the house after him.

The boy gazed around at us with a look of wonder. When he saw me, though, he broke into a wide smile. "It's Nell!" he said to his older sister, grabbing the sleeve of her jacket and shaking it. "Look, Tammany, it's Nell!"

Tammany, who looked like Mrs. Nerriberry in miniature except crabbier, jerked her arm away from him. The girl was not exactly a ray of sunshine, but I was happy to see her anyway. Although maybe that was simply because she wasn't a Magician.

"Where's the big one?" Tammany asked me.

"Crud? He's back home," I told her.

Her eyes passed over the ghosts without a flicker of surprise—I guess she was used to all sorts of creatures traipsing through her home—but she looked squinty eyed at Tom and Lysander.

"Mams!" She turned to her mother with sudden panic when she realized what they were.

"Yes, they're Imps, love, don't stare. Now go and fetch your uncle Reynold." When Tammany opened her mouth to object, Mrs. Nerriberry added, "You can take your dad's boat. And tell Uncle Reynold it's important."

"I'll just tell him there are two Imps at our house," Tammany said dryly.

"Yes, that should do the trick." Mrs. Nerriberry had an amused smile on her face as she watched her daughter leave, slamming the door shut.

"But Tammany was supposed to roll me all the way to Buxton Hill and down it," Jack complained.

Something extraordinary happened then. Samuel rose from his chair by the fire and glided over to Jack. He reached out and touched him, then darted a few yards away and bobbed in place.

"What's it doing?" Jack asked, staring at Samuel.

"He wants to play lurgy fever," Tom said.

"Oh, I love that game!" said Jack.

"Go on, then, go outside and play, all of you!" Mrs. Nerriberry shooed all the ghosts and Jack out the door where, from what I could see out the window, they had immediately launched into some version of tag.

Not twenty minutes later, the door opened again and this time Tammany entered with a short, slump-shouldered man. He was dressed in a thick oatmeal-colored sweater that had seen better days and he wore glasses. His hair was the same messy mop as Mrs. Nerriberry's—and Tammany's, for that matter—except it was definitely thinning on top. He looked like the guy who netted goldfish for you at the pet store. I felt a deflating whoosh of misgiving. If he really was a spy, he was a very under-whelming one. He kept his hands in his pockets and ambled through the door, nodding casually at Lysander and Tom. He looked at me last of all, but I had the feel-ing that of the three of us, I was the one who interested him the most.

"Hoi, Lally," he said to Mrs. Nerriberry. "Keeping busy, I see." There was a faint whiff of disapproval.

"No busier than you, Reynold," Mrs. Nerriberry coun-tered.

"How's the patient?" He nodded toward the skrill, his hands still jammed in his pockets.

"Still out, poor thing. Now have a seat. This child has something to ask you."

Reynold nodded affably and wound his way around the table toward an empty chair, but stopped short in front of me. His hands sprung out of his pockets and he swiftly grabbed my wrist and twisted it. I yelped—more out of surprise than pain.

Tom leapt on his back in an instant and wrapped an arm around his throat, while Lysander jumped up on the table, stepping right into the Iced Nippers, and sprang at Reynold, knocking him to the ground. Reynold had kept hold of my wrist, though, so I went down with him.

"What are you doing, Reynold!" Mrs. Nerriberry shrieked. "Stop it! Stop it now!"

Even with Lysander on top of him, Reynold had managed to maneuver my hand, grunting with the effort to twist his head while in Tom's grip, and stare intently at my palm for a moment.

"Okay, okay, it's fine," he said, his voice throttled by the pressure Tom still had on his throat. Reynold released my wrist, and I scrambled away from him and jumped to my feet, my shoulder throbbing from where it had slammed against the ground. Lysander rolled off Reynold, but Tom kept his arm locked around Reynold's throat.

"I thought you said he was on our side," Tom said to Mrs. Nerriberry, accusingly.

Reynold tried to speak, but Tom's arm must have tightened against his larynx because all he could get out were a few gurgles.

"He is on your side!" Mrs. Nerriberry snapped at Tom. "Give the man half a chance to utter a word and maybe he'll explain himself."

Reluctantly, Tom released him. Reynold gagged loudly, his face the color of a raw T-bone. Slowly he got to his feet, his eyes fixed guardedly on Tom. He took a few deep

breaths, adjusted his glasses, and made a halfhearted attempt
to smooth down his hair.

"A Human with Imp bodyguards?" he said after a
moment, shaking his head in wonder. "That's a first."

"Friends, not bodyguards," I corrected.

"What were you thinking, Reynold? Attacking a child?"
Mrs. Nerriberry demanded.

"I had to make sure she was who she said she was."

"By tackling me?" I asked.

"I didn't mean to . . . I just had to check your life line."

"My what?'

He held up his hand and traced the line that arced from
just above his thumb down toward his wrist. "Magicians
from the Nigh always have triple life lines on the palms of
their hands. Yours just has the one."

"All that fuss and a whole plate of Iced Nippers
destroyed when I could just as well have told you she
wasn't one of them, Reynold." Mrs. Nerriberry righted
her chair in disgust. "You were always overly dra-
matic. . . ."

"A Human and two Imps are in your home," Reynold
fired back in his own defense. "Can you blame me if—"

"They're here because they need our help. This child's
brother is missing. His name is River Batista."

"I've heard about him through . . . through some of my
colleagues. But I don't know where he is."

"I think Mary Carpenter might," I told him. "Do you
know where to find her?"

Reynold's eyes cut over to Mrs. Nerriberry, before he replied sharply, "No."

"This is no time for secrets, Reynold," Mrs. Nerriberry warned.

"I don't know, Lally."

"He doesn't know," said a voice, faint and croaky, that seemed to come from nowhere at all and everywhere too. "But I do."

22

SOLLY

"She's awake!" Mrs. Nerriberry hurried over to the skrill by the fireplace. The little animal had lifted its head, though its whole body trembled with the effort.

"Don't strain yourself, little miss," Mrs. Nerriberry said to the skrill as she crouched down and gently placed a hand on the creature's head.

"How long have I slept?" The hoarse voice came again from nowhere, but now I understood that it was the skrill speaking. I'd had some experience with skrills, so the fact that her voice just sprang into my mind was not surprising. It was how skrills communicated. They didn't speak out loud, but you could hear them in your head. Apparently, her voice also sprang into everyone else's mind too, since Mrs. Nerriberry answered her.

"Since this morning, love. I've stitched you up and you should be good as gold in a few days."

I walked over to the little animal, who watched me with bleary eyes.

"You said you know where Mary Carpenter is?" I asked her.

The skrill tried to get to her feet. I felt an unnerving jolt in my mind, as though I had touched a live electric fence, minus the actual sensation, and I realized I was feeling the animal's surprise at its own pain.

"No, no, keep still!" Mrs. Nerriberry insisted as the skrill stood up and took a few steps. "You're wound is still oozy, and look, you're limping."

"This limp?" I felt a burbling sensation in my mind and I knew the skrill was laughing. "This limp is an old friend. I've forgotten a time when I'd ever walked without her."

I scrutinized the skrill more carefully now. The cagey look in her eyes. The limp.

I had met her before.

"You're Mary Carpenter's skrill!" I cried.

"Mary Carpenter's skrill? Is that my name, I beg your pardon, Mary Carpenter's skrill?" she said huffily, her tail puffing out. "I am my own skrill."

"I'm sorry. What's your name?"

"My name is Solly." The fur on the skrill's tail settled down. "But yes, Mary Carpenter and I have been friends for many years. I've known her since she was a child."

Mrs. Nerriberry let out a fan-girl gasp.

"Several weeks ago," I heard the skrill say in my mind, "Mary told me she had something important to look into. If it had to do with your brother or not, I'm afraid I wouldn't know. She tends to keep things to herself. Safer that way, I suppose, for everyone. Anyway, I'd received word that she was coming back from the Hither soon, so yesterday I went to one of the Wickets that she often uses and that . . . that thing came out of nowhere."

"Now, shhh, you're upsetting yourself," Mrs. Nerriberry said, stroking Solly's back gently.

"I'm worried, I won't lie," the skrill said. "Something odd is happening and there's Mary, traveling between Hither and Nigh. . . .What's the time, please?"

"Half eight," Mrs. Nerriberry replied.

"Right." Solly limped toward the door.

"Where do you think you're going, miss?" Mrs. Nerriberry exclaimed.

"Back to the City. The next Wicket to open is at Pickle Pauli's this afternoon, so that is where I'm headed."

"Nonsense! You're not well enough! You need to rest."

"No time to rest," Solly said. "There are things to do. Don't worry, dear Mrs. Nerriberry, I'm a tough old girl."

"We'll go with her," I said.

I caught Mrs. Nerriberry giving her brother a sharp nudge with her elbow. "You'll go too, Reynold. They're going to need someone to keep an eye on them."

"They seem like they can take care of themselves just fine." He shot a resentful look at Tom and Lysander. He was clearly still smarting from being jumped by a pair of Imps.

She dismissed this with a flick of her hand and turned to us. "He's going."

Solly considered this, then said, "All right, I don't mind the company. Thank you, Mrs. Nerriberry. Perhaps I'll bring Mary to visit with you next time."

This sent Mrs. Nerriberry into such paroxysms of delight that I thought she might drop to her knees in a swoon.

"Imagine Mary Carpenter coming to my home! Ach, this place is a mess! I'll have to tidy . . . although where would I put all my creatures . . . ?" Mrs. Nerriberry fretted.

"Please don't change a thing," Solly said graciously. "There isn't a house in all of the Nigh that could be more charming than Mrs. Nerriberry's cottage."

I agreed, 100 percent.

23

The Journey

We said our goodbyes to Mrs. Nerriberry. The woman was a hugger, so it took a while. Not that I minded. When she hugged Lysander, he said something in her ear. She let him go, then patted his cheek gently.

"They'll need you with them," she said.

Lysander nodded, though I thought his eyes looked damp. So I guessed he had asked if he could stay.

Tom went outside to gather up the ghosts. They were darting all around the yard while Jack chased them, bright flickers of light, pulsing with laughter.

Tom started for them, but Mrs. Nerriberry put a hand on his shoulder to stop him.

"Let them stay," she said.

"Stay here? You mean just leave them?" Tom was clearly appalled at the idea. "But they're mine. I take care of them!"

A look of indignation passed across Mrs. Nerriberry's face. She seemed about to remind Tom that he had put them in considerable danger already, but she must have reconsidered.

"Yes, I know you do," she said. "But think. You'll all be going to who knows where, probably into great danger, not to mention the possibility of being caught out in the rain or there'll be another boat ride. And then what will become of the poor little things?"

Tom didn't answer, but I could see he was thinking about this.

"They'll be well looked after here," Mrs. Nerriberry persisted. "And they'll have Jack to be silly with and Tammany to annoy."

Tom bit at the side of his thumb as he watched Jack chase Samuel around a tree.

"Lurgies!" Jack cried out when his hand swiped at Samuel's light-filled body.

"Katerina has nightmares," Tom said.

"They'll all sleep in Jack and Tammany's bedroom, and I'll be right down the hall to console her," Mrs. Nerriberry assured him.

After a thoughtful pause, Tom frowned and shook his head. "No. I can't just leave them in a strange place."

"Wait," I said. "What if Lysander stays with them? They like him. And if they get too homesick, he can take them back to his island."

Lysander's face brightened at this suggestion. "I wouldn't mind." He looked at Mrs. Nerriberry. "If that's okay with you?"

"Lally," Reynold said to his sister warningly. "An Imp? Living in your house?"

Mrs. Nerriberry shot him a defiant look, then turned to Lysander and replied, "Of course you can stay. We'll be happy to have you."

With Lysander staying, Tom agreed, reluctantly, to let the ghosts stay as well. He wouldn't say goodbye to them though. "They'll just make a whole fuss about it," he said gruffly, but I think he was just worried that he'd change his mind or cry or both.

Mrs. Nerriberry had fashioned a sling for Solly, so that at least she wouldn't have to walk.

"I will not be carried like a sack of beans," Solly said indignantly when she saw the sling.

There was a brief standoff between Solly and Mrs. Nerriberry, but in the end, Mrs. Nerriberry convinced Solly that the group could move more swiftly if they carried her. Reynold wore the sling around his neck and Solly was nestled in snugly against his chest. She sat up very straight, front paws draped over the sling and head held high, like the figurehead of a ship.

"Goodbye, Lysander," I said, and held out my hand. He ignored it and threw his arms around me in a tight hug. "Thank you, Nell, thank you!"

I knew why he was thanking me. I knew he was grateful for the chance to stay with Mrs. Nerriberry in a real home, with a real family. But when he let me go, and saw Reynold looking questioningly at him, he tipped up his chin and said, "I'm thanking her because she put a protection spell on my faering. A powerful one."

Reynold glanced at me. I think he could tell, by the look on my face, that a little white lie might have been told at some point, but he nodded. "Very kind of her."

Reynold led us round the back of Mrs. Nerriberry's house, where we waded through high weedy grass.

"Don't we have to go back through the canal?" I asked.

"Too dangerous to go to the City from that direction. Most of those ships in the City's harbor are owned by the Minister, or Folk who work closely with her. We don't need any attention from the crews."

I shot Tom a look. Too late for that.

The high weeds gave way to a field, speckled with sheep. The largest one eyed us suspiciously and hurried away, followed by the rest of the flock, a mass of fat wooly white bodies jogging on their peg legs. From her sling, Solly called commands: "Watch the pile of droppings there!" "We ought to move faster."

We came to an expanse of waist-high stalks of some bristly crop that I couldn't identify. It had recently been cut back. The ground beneath us was soft with spent, slippery husks, and the tops of those plants were stiff and sharp. And I'm a klutz. We weren't in there for more than a few minutes before my chin was bleeding where one of the plants had stabbed me when I slipped, and there were painful, razor-thin slices on my hands.

"Maybe we could go back to the fields, where things are less stabby," I said to Reynold.

"This way's shorter," Reynold replied tersely.

After what seemed like ages, we finally emerged and found ourselves in a clearing of scruffy brush and stunted trees. Just ahead of us was a dark stone house, flanked on one side by a tiny graveyard with a half dozen leaning headstones. Next to the house was a large, hexagon-shaped building with huge, planked doors. Its outer walls were covered in dried mud and its roof was thatched with that same hairy stuff as some of the cottage roofs.

As soon as we approached the buildings, a flock of angry geese ran at us, pumping their heads up and down and hissing. The barn door was flung open and a large man appeared, holding a very nasty-looking machete. His face was cinched in like a drawstring bag, his brows pulled down, and his thin lips bunching up under his nose. He took us all in while I kept my eyes on that machete. When the man spotted Reynold, though, his face relaxed. It still wasn't exactly friendly, but at least he no longer looked like he wanted to behead us.

"Sorry about that," he said to Reynold. "The neighbor down aways said she saw something shuffling though the orchards this morning. A Grubble probably. Them things is getting bolder and bolder, poking around in broad daylight."

"A pack of pests," agreed Reynold. "How's it, Griffin?"

"Not bad. My left knee's been giving me trouble." His eyes passed over Tom and me again. "Interesting company you're keeping these days, I see." On noticing Solly, his eyes lit up with surprise. "Ah! You're a skrill! We don't see many of your kind around here." He put his hand on his heart and bowed his head. "Pleased to meet you, madam." I had no idea how he knew Solly was a madam and not a sir, but his cordiality seemed to make up for the indignity of riding in a pouch.

"The pleasure is all mine," she replied, like a very small queen.

Tom leaned over to me and whispered nervously, "Do you smell it?"

I sniffed the air. There was a faint musky odor.

"I smell something," I said.

"So," the man, Griffin, said to Reynold, "what do you need today?" His eyes shifted to me, sizing me up. "Two Molossers?"

"Three," Reynold replied.

Griffin seemed to think this was hysterical. "Well," he said when he'd finished laughing, his eyes squarely on Tom. "This should be interesting."

He turned and headed back into the hexagonal building he'd come out of. As the door opened, I was hit by a powerful burst of that musky smell, as well as a chorus of growls and yelps.

"I'm not going in there," Tom said, crossing his arms over his chest and planting his feet.

"Eh! You're being a baby." Reynold mussed Tom's hair and walked past him, into the building.

"What's in there, Tom?" I asked. I wasn't sure I wanted to go in either, frankly.

Tom didn't answer. The "baby" comment seemed to have gotten to him. He smoothed his hair down, scowling, and walked through the door.

24

DOGGES

Listen, I'd seen some surprising things over the past couple of weeks, but what I saw in the barn made me say something straight out of a cartoon speech bubble: "What the—? Whoa!"

Inside the barn were a series of stalls, the upper halves of which had barred openings. In each stall were tremendous dogs, some pacing, some shoving their noses between the bars. I know you'll sometimes hear people say, "That dog is as big as a horse." But these dogs were *exactly* as big as a horse. Some of them were even bigger.

"Dogges," Reynold said to me when he saw my face, pronouncing the word as "dowgs."

"Right. Dogges."

The last time I'd been in the Nigh, I'd seen the Magicians riding them, but always at a distance. Up close was a different story. These were massive beasts, with thick bunchy muscles and heads like cement blocks. They also looked nothing like the ones I'd seen before. The dogges that the Magicians rode were elegant creatures, lithe and long-legged. They had—and I know it's weird to say—aristocratic faces. The dogges in this barn were more of the junkyard variety.

From their stalls, the dogges eyeballed us, their huge damp noses quivering as they took in our smells. A low growl rumbled from the stall closest to us. A black-furred behemoth was staring at Tom as its upper lip twitched spasmodically, exposing a set of shark teeth, in candy corn gradations of yellow, orange, and white.

Griffin laughed as he reached his hand between the bars and scratched the dogge behind its ear.

"Her name is Bluebell. What do you say, Imp?" Griffin nodded at Tom. "You want to ride her?"

"Pass," Tom said, standing well away from her stall.

"Go on," Griffin said. "She's not so tough. She just needs to get to know you. Just give her some sweet talk. You Imps know how to do that."

Tom looked at me in a "should I or shouldn't I?" way.

"Let her smell you at least. I mean, they are dogs," I said. "Sort of."

Tom nodded, though I saw his throat tick as he swallowed back his nerves. Slowly, he approached Bluebell's stall. The growling grew louder, like stones grinding against each other. Bluebell's twitching upper lip was well above her gumline, a raised curtain at a fang show.

"Hey, girl," Tom said hesitantly.

The dogge stopped growling. Her upper lip dropped back over her teeth and her nostrils shuttered in and out as she took audible sniffs. Tom put his hand close to the bars for her to smell. She stretched out her neck toward it.

"That's a good girl, Bluebell," Tom cooed. "Nice dogge. Look at those big brown eyes of yours."

He reached his hand between the bars. In a split second, Bluebell lunged at him, slamming her chest against the stall's door and snapping her terrifying choppers, missing Tom's hand by the width of an eyelash.

I felt a warm dribble of liquid on my shoulder. Winston. That Willaweeper had a really gnarly sense of humor.

"Settle!" Griffin bellowed at Bluebell, which stopped her on a dime. "Don't worry, Imp. She'll behave once you get her going." He turned to Reynold, grinning, and with a side-of-the-mouth whisper said, "Either that or you'll be picking Imp bones out of her teeth."

Reynold didn't smile back. Maybe that was a little too close to the truth.

"Go on, girl," Griffin said to me. "Choose your ride. I'd stick to them over there if I were you." He nodded toward the far side of the stable.

The dogges there were smaller, but only slightly. I heard squealing in one of the stalls and peered through the bars to see a litter of massive biscuit-colored pups nursing. They were so young that their eyes were still sealed shut, but their mom was glaring at me warily. I walked alongside the stalls, looking for the smallest possible dogge. I'd never ridden a horse in my life, and I generally have trouble staying upright on flat surfaces. Also I'm not a fan of heights.

Like, it's verging on a phobia. Staying as close to the ground as possible seemed wise.

I stopped at the sight of a dogge who was curled on a bed of straw in the corner of the stall. A dun-colored dogge with a pink nose, he looked slightly less barrel-chested than some of the others. One ear was upright while the other one folded down. He stared back at me and his tail thumped the ground cautiously.

"This one," I called over to Griffin, who was in the stall with Bluebell, cinching a saddle around her belly.

Griffin looked over at me and frowned. "Wallace? Nah, you don't want that one. Plum useless. I'll be putting him down in a day or so."

If I was on the fence before, this decided it for me. "I want Wallace," I insisted. "Definitely."

Griffin looked over at Reynold to back him up, but it was Solly who spoke. "The girl has good instincts. Let her choose."

"If you say so," Griffin said resignedly. "Wallace is hers." He turned to Reynold. "I'm guessing you'll want Horst, as usual."

"He hasn't failed me yet," Reynold said.

Huge and gray, with cat-yellow eyes, Horst was an impressive beast. He was covered with fine, white scars, long healed but hinting at a violent past.

"Rescued him," Griffin said when he caught me looking at the dogge's scars. "The Magicians had used him to fight their own dogges for entertainment. Of course, they only had him fight the dogges that they didn't want anymore, since Horst never lost. He's a good one, though. Got eyes in the back of his head. Knows what you want before you know it yourself."

Griffin saddled up all the dogges. The bridles didn't have mouth bits, like they would on a horse, but instead were attached to a thin leather band that looped beneath the dogges' throats and attached to a strap just behind their ears.

Griffin boosted me up on Wallace's back. I didn't love the feeling of being so high off the ground, but at least Wallace stood quietly while I adjusted to find my balance.

Getting Tom on Bluebell was a whole other story.

The dogge seemed to have a real aversion to him. Every time Tom tried to get on Bluebell, the animal would whip around with bared teeth and swivel her body away.

"It's the smell," Griffin confided to me, touching the side of his nose. "They can smell that Imps aren't regular Folk. It spooks 'em."

"The Imp is harmless, Bluebell." We all heard Solly's commanding voice in our minds.

"You can speak to dogges?" I asked Solly.

"Does that surprise you?"

"I guess it shouldn't."

Solly's assurance seemed to do the trick. Bluebell calmed down enough to let Tom sit on her. But as soon as he slipped his feet in the stirrups and gathered up the reins, Bluebell appeared to have second thoughts. She rammed her back end into the side of the barn in an effort to dislodge him. When he kept his seat, she whipped her head around to clamp her teeth onto his knee. Tom was too quick for her though. He grabbed the scruff of her neck with both hands and gave it a sharp yank, which surprised her enough to stop her antics.

"Well done, Tom!" Reynold said, clearly impressed. It was the first time I'd heard Reynold call Tom by his name.

After that, Bluebell behaved herself for the most part, though as we headed out, she broke into a hair-raising run, with Tom holding on for dear life. Thankfully, Tom had exceptionally good balance. Bluebell finally lost interest in ditching him and trotted along with the rest of the dogges like a champ.

We traveled through fields that were mercifully flat. Reynold in the lead gradually picked up the pace, until we were full-on galloping. Or whatever the equivalent of galloping is for a dogge. In any case, my heart was kicking with nerves, but I had to admit the sensation was thrilling. My dogge Wallace wasn't nearly as fast as the other dogges. Maybe he could feel that I was balance-impaired and was being extra careful. He had a nice steady gait and he ran so smoothly that I felt as though I were just sitting on a floating chair, the wind whipping my braids back as the landscape flew by. We had just passed a large herd of goats when Reynold called out "Hisshhht!"

The dogges stopped so quickly that I would have

tumbled right over Wallace's head if he hadn't lifted his neck to block me.

Tom and I looked over at Reynold for an explanation. He put a finger to his lips, then pointed. Up ahead was another field of those awful stabby plant stalks. It took me a moment to spot what Reynold was pointing at: some of the stalks were moving, even though the air was still, without even the smallest breeze.

"Ishhh!" Reynold said to Horst. Horst's ears pivoted forward. His whole body stiffened. He lowered his head, then pinned his ears back. He was like an arrow drawn against the bow, just waiting to be released so it could skewer its target.

"Is it a Grubble?" I whispered to Tom.

He nodded. "I think so."

I guess if I was on foot, I would have been afraid. But high up on Wallace's back, and with that maniac Bluebell beside me, hackles raised, I only felt a thrilling tingle of anticipation. I was going to see a Sasquatch. An actual Sasquatch.

25

ᵀHE ᵀRAVELERS

The stalks shifted again and this time I saw a flash of red cloth. Horst must have seen it too, because I could see his muscles twitching.

"Not a Grubble," Tom whispered.

"Magician?" I asked, but Reynold turned around and shot me a warning look to shut up.

I saw a hand reach up above one of the stalks to push it aside. Another hand appeared, behind the first, to fend off the stalk that had snapped backward.

So there were two of them, at least.

"Let me do the talking." I heard Solly's voice in my head. "Don't try to run. Not yet."

I reached for my chopsticks, even though the only spell I had that might truly stop a Magician in its tracks was the one that I didn't ever want to use again.

Wallace let out a soft whine.

"Shh, it's okay," I whispered to him, and stroked his neck.

The stalks at the edge of the field parted and two

people appeared, both looking worse for the wear. Their clothes and shoes were caked with dried mud, and their faces were masks of exhaustion.

"Annika! Crud!" I called out in shock.

I don't know if it was the tone of my voice—excitement bordering on hysterics—or the fact that, at the sight of the three huge beasts facing them, Annika and Crud had whipped out their chopsticks. In any case, Horst was the first one to charge at them, followed closely by Bluebell.

"Stop!" I shrieked. "*Stop!* They're friends!" But Wallace and I were too far behind Reynold for him to hear me.

Tom was pulling back on Bluebell's reins with all his might and I could see her beginning to slow her pace, but Horst was bearing down on Annika and Crud, his head thrust forward and his teeth bared. Crud was already beginning to work a spell—probably some sort of ward— which most definitely wasn't going to help his case with Reynold.

"We know them, we know them!" Tom shouted at Reynold.

Reynold must have heard him, because he suddenly jerked back on Horst's reins and called out, "Hooooo, boy!" Horst stopped so quickly that he reared up, his great fore-legs with claws the size of railroad spikes pawing at the air as he towered over a terrified Crud and Annika. When his legs came back down on the ground, he let out one sharp bark but stayed put.

Annika and Crud still had their chopsticks raised, but

the sparks from Crud's spell were already dying and falling into the grass. They gawked at us, clearly trying to make sense of what they were seeing.

"Why are you two riding on hellhounds?" Crud asked.

"They're dogges," I said. "How did you get here?"

"The hard way," Annika replied.

Yeah, it looked like the two of them had been chewed up, spit out, and trampled on. Crud's hair was clumped up on one side, and I thought I saw a few burdocks lodged in it.

"But how did you know where to find us?" I asked.

"I figured you might wind up in Piddlebank," Crud said. "Mrs. Nerriberry and all."

"Mrs. Nerriberry doesn't live far from here," Reynold said brusquely. "Just follow this field past those goats and you'll come to a large barn. Take the next field and it will lead you straight to her place. It will be tricky to find a usable Wicket the way things are now, but I'll send someone over, and with any luck, they can help you get back home."

"We're not going back home," Crud said flatly. "We're going with Nell."

"Absolutely not," Reynold said. "I can't babysit three Humans."

"Hey, Glasses!" Annika stepped forward so that she was nose-to shoulder with Horst. She glared up at Reynold. "I've been taking care of myself since I was four. And just look at him!" She jerked a thumb toward Crud. "You think he can't handle himself as well as you can? Better, by the looks of you."

"Annika!" I warned sharply. I turned to Reynold. "These are our friends. The last time the four of us were in the Nigh, the Minister tried to drop an entire apartment building on our heads, and I'm pretty sure if any one of us hadn't been there, she would have succeeded. They need to come with us."

"And what are they going to ride?" Reynold countered.

"The dogges say they're willing to carry them too." It was Solly's voice that erupted in my head. In everyone else's heads too, because Annika and Crud looked around for whoever was speaking.

"Wait," Annika said to me. "Who's talking?"

"She is." I pointed at Solly in the sling, who stretched her neck up so that Annika could get a good look at her.

"*That?*" Annika cried. "The gremlin in the BabyBjörn?"

I felt a burbly sensation in my chest. Apparently, so did Annika.

"What is that?" Annika cried out, her hand on her own chest. "It's like someone just opened a can of soda with my rib cage!"

"That's because you made Solly laugh," I said.

"Really?" Annika looked over at Solly, whose large brown eyes stared back. "Well, obviously she has a great sense of humor."

Reynold told Crud to ride on Bluebell, since she was a big dogge, while Annika would ride on Wallace with me.

I put out my hand to help Annika up onto Wallace, but she ignored it and swung herself onto Wallace's back, no problem.

Crud walked right up to Bluebell and held out his hand for her to sniff.

"Don't!" Tom warned, and I half expected Bluebell to take his hand off for him, but she surprised us both by snuffling at his palm curiously. Crud scratched her beneath her chin and Bluebell's tail actually wagged.

"Tell you what," Tom said, scooching back in the saddle. "She obviously likes you better than me, so why don't you drive."

Crud took to riding Bluebell easily and it wasn't long before we were all trotting together at a decent pace.

"How did you find a Wicket anyway?" I asked.

"When you didn't come back at the street fair," Crud said, "we figured something went wrong. Or as Annika kindly put it, 'What kind of a mess did Nell get herself into now?'"

"Our Floopers were a piece of cake, by the way," Annika said.

"So we headed over to Skull 'n Bones to see what had happened. When we spotted the Anywhere Taxi up on the sidewalk, we started running, but by the time we got there and opened the taxi door . . . no you. We didn't have a token or anything, so the driver wasn't going to take us, but then Annika had the bright idea of mentioning Vanessa's name. That did the trick. We told him to take us to where you went. He said, 'Don't tell me how to do my job.' The next thing we knew, he had dumped us in the middle of nowhere."

"Tossed us out so fast that I left my briefcase in the taxi," Annika groused.

"At least the Fates are back in the Nigh, where they belong," Crud told her.

"Aaanyway." Annika rolled her eyes.

"We had no idea where we were, so we just walked for hours," Crud continued.

"Correction, we walked in a circle for hours."

"Yeah," Crud admitted. "Turns out, without street signs, neither one of us can find our way out of a paper bag. Anyway, we eventually ran into this lady who was hunting for mushrooms. She was really decent. She took us to her place and fed us, and told us that we were in Brooklyn. So of course, I thought of Mrs. Nerriberry. It was already dark though, so she let us sleep at her place, and in the morning she gave us directions to Piddlebank. Which, as you can see by our clothes, included walking through a swamp."

Annika snorted. "A swamp. In Brooklyn."

As it turned out, there were plenty of other swamps in Brooklyn too, and it felt like we hit every single one of them once we passed the fields. The dogges waded through the muck, stepping slowly and carefully until we got to dry land where they could break into a trot again.

At one point we came upon a little village on the edge

of a forest. We passed a man driving a rattly wooden cart, pulled by a dogge with fur so long and bedraggled that it looked like the cart was being towed by a giant mop. The man in the cart waved to us and smiled, flashing a mouthful of gums. The houses in this village were in bad shape. Most of them were little more than mud-and-stick shacks, sprawled haphazardly along a network of narrow dirt roads.

This was where we saw an actual Grubble. At first I thought it was a bear because it was on all fours, digging furiously at a row of vegetables planted in back of one of the shacks. But as we passed, it lifted its head, and I saw its face. Set in his primate features were eerily human eyes that gazed back at us as it shoved a handful of lettuce in its mouth.

"Dude, that's a Bigfoot!" Crud said.

"Grubble," I corrected, "but basically the same thing."

Just then a man came running out of the house in front of the garden and threw a bottle at the Grubble. The Grubble stood up—his head was as tall as the house's roof—and lumbered off to the garden next door, leaving a gaping hole in the earth where the vegetables had been. No wonder Folk couldn't stand them.

We had just passed through the village and were back into open fields once more when I heard Winston's alarm in my ear: "*Wickle-wickle-feee! Wickle-wickle-feee!*"

"What was that?" Annika was sitting right behind me, so she heard the alarm too.

"There's something dangerous nearby," I told the others.

"How do you know?" Reynold asked.

I hesitated, glancing over at Crud. "I have a Willaweeper in my hair."

"Nell!" Crud cried.

"Vanessa gave it to me, okay?" I said. "And anyway, you should be glad I have it because it's giving us a warning."

"How close is the danger?" Reynold asked. His voice was remarkably calm, while I, on the other hand, was already feeling nauseous with fear.

"Well, if I'm going by the last few times Winston sounded the alarm," I replied, "it's close enough so that we should be worrying."

With a "Chaaaa!" Reynold urged Horst on at a faster clip and Bluebell and Wallace followed suit. After a few minutes, I heard Solly's urgent voice in my head: "It's a Magician."

"Are you kidding me?" Annika cried.

"How do you know?" I called to Solly.

"The dogges know," Solly replied.

I looked down at Wallace. He had plastered his ears against his head, and the hairs on his back were standing straight up in a bristly line.

"Right. Hang on!" Reynold abruptly pulled Horst's reins to the left and shouted "Chaaa! Chaaa!" urging the dogge into an all-out sprint. Bluebell chased after him, making Crud and Tom pitch backward in the saddle. Wallace ran too, but was slower to get up to full speed. In a few moments, we were racing so fast that even Annika reached around and held on to my waist. For some reason that made me feel the tiniest bit braver.

26

THE BRIDGE

We sprinted across the fields until the grass was gradually overtaken by clumps of reeds and low-growing shrubs, and the ground turned soft and mucky. Here and there were lonely stands of huddled trees. The dogges were forced to slow down to a walk as their paws struggled to lift out of the sucking mud. There was a spooky stillness here, a sense of things lying in wait, hidden in the sludge. At the same time, I kept searching the sky for signs of a Magician, so I felt sandwiched between threats, above and below.

The land gradually rose and became drier, the trees taller, and we abruptly arrived at the banks of a gently moving river. Across the way, we could see the City's skyline. Most of the tall buildings were bunched up farther north, so that the island looked like a mouth with its front teeth missing.

On this side of the river, the bank was deserted except for a large wooden pier that jutted out into the water, rising and falling with the currents. Oddly, someone had built a shack right on top of the pier. Its roof was flat and pierced by a crooked chimney, and its windows were so warped that cloth had been shoved in the cracks. It was hard to believe anyone lived in that thing, but there were voices and music coming from inside.

Reynold dismounted from Horst and began to untie a canvas sack that hung from his saddle.

"Should we really be stopping now?" I asked him nervously.

"We won't be long. And Magicians avoid this place if they can."

The rest of us dismounted too. My butt was aching and my back was feeling all jangly from being on Wallace for so long. The dogges shook themselves off, making their saddles slap around on their backs.

From the canvas sack, Reynold pulled out several pieces of meat, then whistled. The dogges dashed over and, after a quick tussle and an explosion of growls, they each dragged off a slab of meat and started gnawing on it.

"Got any steaks in there for people?" Crud asked.

Reynold ignored the question. "Wait here."

He removed Solly's sling and placed her gently on the ground, then headed over to the shack on the pier.

Solly shuffled off to pee along the edge of some shrubs, not bothering with privacy, but we all looked away anyhow.

"Why does this place feel so familiar?" Crud asked, gazing around.

"Well, there's that." I pointed to the City.

"No, I mean this particular spot," Crud said. "There's something about it."

He was right. There was something oddly familiar about the place, though I couldn't think why.

"Yeah," Annika said. "It is familiar. It just feels like it's missing something."

"Exactly," I said.

"Yeah, like, it's missing something kind of large." The snark was creeping into Annika's voice. "Something with lots of cables and maybe a bike path—"

"The Brooklyn Bridge!" Crud and I both said at once.

"Who says these two are slow?" Annika quipped to Tom.

"You do, mostly," he replied.

"We had a bridge here once too," said Solly, who had finished her business and was limping back to us. "Many years ago."

"What happened to it?" I asked.

"Ah. Now, there's a story." Solly sat back on her haunches, adjusting her bad leg so that it was settled at an awkward angle. I could see the stitched-up gash on her side. It looked raw and oozy, and I worried that the trip had made it worse.

"Brooklyn has always been a place where Folk live in the old ways, the way they do in Piddlebank. The Minister isn't happy about that. She's keen on expanding her power beyond the City, into the boroughs. Many years ago, she decided to build a bridge connecting Brooklyn to the City. She had a Human child cast it, and when it was done, the Minister held a huge celebration on the bridge. Lots of fanfare. Thousands of Folk came to see it. There were bands playing music on the bridge. Ships on the river below set off fireworks. When the Minister made her appearance, she walked out on the bridge, holding hands with the Human child who had created it. Everyone went wild with applause. Speeches were made. Various Magicians were honored for their loyalty to the Minister, that sort of nonsense. And then it happened."

Solly paused. Her words now turned to images in our minds. It was like watching footage of a silent movie in your brain. I could see the bridge now. It was a beautiful creation, nearly an exact replica of the Brooklyn Bridge that I knew. I could see crowds of Folk on the banks flanking the bridge, though mostly on the City's side, holding banners. On the bridge itself was the band, and in the middle of the bridge were a bunch of Magicians. They wore their usual drab office clothing, with ceremonial blue banners crossing their chests.

Standing on a podium at the center of the bridge was the Minister herself. She was talking, though I couldn't hear her words.

"Oh man," Crud groaned. "Now, there's a face I'd be happy to never see again."

I felt my nerves bristle at the sight of the Minister, even if she was only a picture in my brain. She was a chubby little girl in glasses, wearing a green ball gown. At least she looked like a little girl, though she was, in fact, extraordinarily old.

By her side was a pale, lanky blond Human girl. The girl looked older than the Minister, though she was probably only twelve or so. Her face was thin and tired looking. She was dressed in a glittery white gown, but there was no sense of celebration in her posture. Her spine was bent and her shoulders slumped with fatigue. Suddenly, she turned her head, and it looked as if she was gazing directly at me. She smiled, a small, sad smile. And that's when it happened. The bridge broke apart. It simply crumbled. The band, the Magicians, the Minister, and the Human girl plummeted straight down into the river. It was shocking and horrific, and I was suddenly glad that there was no sound in my brain. Or maybe Solly had tried to spare us the screams. Then the image went black.

"How did that happen?" I asked Solly.

"No one knows. Many lives were lost that day."

"But the Minister survived."

"She survived, obviously. And a handful of others."

"What about the kid?" Crud asked.

"Died with the rest of them. The currents were strong that day. It swept them away. In any case, the bridge was never rebuilt. And more to the point, this part of the river is often avoided by Magicians. Superstition, I suppose. Which means it is the best place to cross to the City, should someone wish to cross in secret."

27

THE WAGER

"Hoi!" Reynold had stepped out of the shack on the pier and gestured for us to come. I bent to pick up Solly, but she ignored me and limped up to the shack herself.

A slender young woman with boyishly cut dark hair and a pointy nose greeted us at the door, nodding to each of us in turn.

The shack, it turned out, was a makeshift pub. There were a dozen or so Folk inside, sitting at tables and drinking what looked an awful lot like watery beer. A few of them were playing cards and there was some sort of board game happening in the corner. The place had been filled with talking and laughter when we opened the door, but as soon as we walked in, every head turned and the ruckus melted into silence.

"We're taking them 'crost, Jasper," said the woman.

"No we ain't, Kells," said a completely bald man with a grizzled chin. He didn't even look up from the board game he'd been playing, shoving a piece forward with his pinky knuckle.

"And so we are." The woman, Kells, was clearly used to getting her way, but the man didn't budge. He just ignored her and kept playing.

"I can pay you twice the fare, to compensate for the dogges," said Reynold.

"I don't care about the dogges," the man named Jasper said to Reynold.

"Then what's the problem?"

Jasper raised his eyes and he looked at Tom. "No Imps on my ferry."

I glanced over at Tom. He didn't even flinch. I guess he was used to this kind of thing, which broke my heart.

"This particular Imp is okay," Reynold insisted.

"None of them are okay," Jasper shot back. "Liars and thieves, the whole lot of them. It's in their blood. You take this one 'crost to the City and he'd sell your Humans to the Magicians without an eye bat, don't think he won't."

Jasper's opponent muttered his agreement with this before moving his game piece.

"He would never do that!" I cried.

"I'm not risking my reputation—" Jasper started.

"Not much of a risk, from the looks of this place," Annika spat out snidely.

"Get them out of here!" Jasper roared at Reynold, jumping to his feet. He wasn't a tall guy but he was burly, and he held himself like a bear about to lunge. Crud stepped forward, ready to meet the threat, but Solly's voice sounded in our heads: "Settle down!"

I felt a pressing urge to take a deep breath, then another. I glanced at Crud. A moment before he had looked ready to storm into battle, but now his shoulders had relaxed, his expression more composed. This was Solly's doing, I was sure if it. She was slipping into our minds, helping us to keep our cool.

"Now listen, my friend," Reynold said to Jasper, his tone light. "You and I aren't strangers. We've done business together before."

"Well, not this time," he said, his eyes on Tom. "That group of yours stinks of trouble."

"You don't—" Reynold started, but Jasper pointed to the door.

"Out!" Jasper stared down Reynold with such ferocity that I saw Reynold take a step back.

If this guy wouldn't take us across now, we'd probably never make it to the City, not with a Magician on our tail. I tried to think of something to say, something that would convince him. My eyes landed on the game he was playing. I'd never seen anything like it before. The board was shaped like a blocky capital I with a grid of black and yellow squares. The playing pieces were made of painted clay, each with different notches along their sides.

"I'll play you," I said to Jasper, nodding toward the board game.

There was some general chuckling, and shouts of "Look out, Jasper, the girl might be a Rounder!" "She'll win the ferry straight off you, Jasp!"

"If I win," I said, "you take us."

I saw something flash across his face. It was a look I'd seen many times before at the chess tables in Washington Square Park. This guy was a gambler. I felt a little ping of hope.

Jasper clasped his hands and tapped his thumbs together, considering.

"And if I win," he said, "I get your dogges."

"They're not ours to give," Reynold piped up.

"Oh, I'm sure you can pay the owner what they're worth," Jasper replied.

"There's three of them, Jasper," said a man who had gone to the window to have a look at the dogges. "But only two of the animals are worth anything."

"We'll use the other one for meat," Jasper said.

Wallace.

I wavered for a minute, but shook it off.

If I know anything about anything it's chess. Chess is basically two brains in a fistfight, and this Jasper guy did not look like a mental heavyweight. True, I didn't recognize the board game on the table, but it had squares and moveable pieces and I'm a quick learner.

"Deal." I started toward the table, but Reynold put a hand on my shoulder to stop me.

"This is a stupid risk."

I turned to look at him. "I'm good at games," I said softly.

He hesitated, but something in my voice must have convinced him, because he nodded and stepped back.

The man who had been playing Jasper gave me his seat with a smirk and a ceremonial flourish.

I looked up at Jasper. "So how do you play this thing?"

That made Jasper bust out laughing. "She's made her wager and she don't even know how to play!"

The others also thought this was hysterical.

"Okay, ha, ha," I said. "Now explain the rules."

He did. They were simple enough. It was all about one player overtaking another, with almost no element of luck involved. My favorite kind of game. It took me exactly five moves to beat him. It should have been four, but I didn't want to piss him off.

Jasper stared at the board for a solid minute, probably trying to figure out if I had tricked him somehow. Then he looked up at me, questioningly. I worried that he might accuse me of cheating somehow and toss us out. The whole place was silent, watching us.

He held out his hand.

"Good game."

I let out a breath, which I had been holding in a state of dread, and shook his hand.

"So you'll take us?"

"I don't worm out of my wagers," Jasper said.

I glanced over at Tom, who smiled at me. I'd won loads of chess games in the park, but none of them had made me as happy as winning this one.

28

THE CROSSING

"So where's the ferry?" Crud asked.

"You're standing on it," Kells, the woman with the short dark hair, told him.

It turned out that the pier was in fact nothing more than an extra-large raft, and when Jasper untied its moorings, the pier floated straight into the river, shack and all, guided by Jasper and another man armed with long oars. The dogges stayed on the raft, outside the shack, though Wallace pressed his nose against the window to stare at me mournfully.

Thankfully the river was calm and the crossing was smooth. I played a few more rounds of the game with three other guys who wanted to make their own wagers. I beat them all, and this time I didn't try to be nice about it. I wound up with a pocket full of coins and some candies wrapped in newspaper.

We were each given a bowl of soup and bread, which was a lucky thing since we hadn't eaten for a while. Solly was given a plate of nuts that she ate with dainty precision.

They gave her some of the beer too, which she lapped out of a bowl. It made her so tipsy that she was singing songs about skrills sailing in a bathtub. She must have been singing in everyone's head because a woman took out an instrument that looked like a cross between a guitar and a surfboard and began to play.

"Come on, Nell, dance with me!" Tom said.

I'd been playing one of the younger guys on the ferry, who wasn't half bad at the game, but when Tom asked me to dance, the guy knocked his piece over. "Forfeit." He winked at Tom, who grinned back at him, so how could I say no, really?

I got up. Tom took my hand in his and placed his other hand on my back.

"O-kaay," I said uncertainly.

We started to dance slowly. Well, Tom was dancing. I was more or less shuffling around.

"FYI, I dropped out of dance class when I was eight," I said. "The teacher literally told my dad that I might have a Left-Right Confusion Disorder."

Tom didn't say anything. He just looked at me and smiled, which made me super nervous. And when I'm nervous, I talk a lot.

"She wasn't kidding either," I said. "Left-Right Confusion Disorder is a real thing."

"I think you're amazing," Tom said.

"Why? Because I'm good at board games?" I flicked him on his forehead. It was a weird thing to do, but I'd never danced with a boy before and it was all really uncomfortable.

His expression turned serious, and for a moment I thought he was mad or something. But then he gently pulled me in close. In a funny way, this made everything feel less awkward. I didn't have to look at his face and wonder why on earth he'd be dancing with me in the first place. I draped my hand around his neck, the way I'd seen people do in movies, and we moved in a little two-step, so slow that even I could manage it. I could feel his breath against my ear and it made me laugh.

"Sorry, Sorry!" I said. "Your breath is tickling my ear."

I am officially ridiculous when it comes to this stuff. I looked around for Annika, who I was sure must be rolling her eyes by now at the sight of me, but thankfully she was busy talking to Crud.

"I'll point my face the other way," Tom said.

"No, don't—just—just keep your face where it is." I shifted my head so that my ear was closer to his neck. I was so conscious of his hand on my back that I half expected it would leave a print on my skin when he took it away. The whole thing made me feel so melty that I rested my head against his shoulder and closed my eyes. I wasn't sure what we were to each other exactly. I definitely thought about him a lot. He lit up the dark corners of my mind. He made my heart race and my face flush red, and yes, I had a big stupid crush on him. But we lived in two separate worlds. I mean, he wasn't even a human boy.

As though he knew what I was thinking, he said quietly,

in the saddest voice, "I wish I wasn't an Imp."

I stopped dancing, drew back, and looked up at him. "Don't say that. I like that you're an Imp. I just wish you lived in the same actual world as I do."

The music changed to a fast, rowdy song, and a moment later Annika slammed into us, jostling us apart.

"Break it up, you two, we're not at the prom." She gestured for Crud to join us on the dance floor as the whole place erupted with the sound of Folk stamping their feet and clapping to the music.

Annika, Crud, Tom, and I all danced together like goofballs. We were having so much fun that, when the ferry bounced against something with a thud, it took us all by surprise. The music stopped. Everyone on the ferry fell silent.

"I guess we're here," Crud said.

We stared out the window at the banks of the City as the ferry bobbed against the pilings. The mood sunk like an anchor. The last time all four of us had been in the City together, we had nearly not made it out alive.

We all filed out of the shack as our shoulders were slapped cheerily and good luck was wished on us by the ferry Folk. Wallace was so thrilled to see me again that he licked one whole side of my head while his backside waggled so vigorously that the whole raft bobbed up and down. I reached up and rubbed his chin, and wondered how hard it would be to keep a dog the size of a horse in our apartment back home.

"We've heard disturbing rumors about the City lately,"

Jasper said to Reynold as we got ready to disembark. "Folk say there are strange creatures roaming the streets."

Reynold nodded. "I've heard the rumors."

Jasper grunted, his eyes on Reynold as though he were sizing him up. "You must have a good reason for taking these youngsters there."

"I do."

Jasper grunted again. Then he stuck out his hand and Reynold shook it.

"She's a clever girl," Jasper said, inclining his head toward me. "I'd like another go at beating her, so you make sure she comes back in one piece. Understand?"

Kells came outside, carrying a bundle of shawls, and handed them to Reynold.

"The Humans will want to cover themselves in the City."

"Thanks, Kells," he said.

She gave Reynold a long look that made me wonder if they knew each other better than I'd thought.

We got on our dogges and headed north along the banks of the East River, where the wind rose up from the water and hissed at us, like a warning that all of us were determined to ignore.

29

PICKLE PAULI'S WICKET

"The Wicket isn't far from here," Solly said. "We should be okay as long as we stay in this part of the City. The Magicians don't tend to come down here."

"I can see why," I said.

The riverbank was apparently being used as a garbage dump. The shore was strewn with rotting food and, worse, fish heads. The smell of dead fish was so powerful I could taste it. I think it even bothered Wallace because he was snuffling and shaking his head as if to dislodge the smell from his nose.

I kept expecting to hear Winston's alarm, but for now, thank goodness, he was silent. It appeared that we had managed to lose the Magician back in Brooklyn.

"This part of the City was one of the first to be casted by Human children," Solly said. "That was many years ago. Of course, the children created what they knew—the tenement buildings they'd lived in back home, the cobbled streets. It was a step up from the wilderness that was here before, so the richer Folk bought the homes from the

Magicians, and the Magicians grew richer themselves, and more powerful. As the years went by, new stolen children casted skyscrapers and smooth sidewalks and fancy stores. The things they knew back home. The 'better things,' some would say."

"Some," Reynold said scornfully. "Not most Folk. Most Folk want to live like we do in Piddlebank, the way Folk have lived for centuries."

"True," Solly said. "But as long as there are other Folk chasing wealth, there will be Magicians chasing power. And the poor Human children are caught in between."

Up ahead I could see the beginnings of actual streets, with lines of brick tenement buildings squashed together and Folk milling around.

"The Wicket is close," said the skrill. "But we'll have to pass through the streets now."

"Put on the shawls," Reynold said. "Cover your faces as much as possible."

We turned the dogges toward the cobblestone streets and rode past the old tenement buildings. Folk were sitting on the tenements' front steps, chatting, while kids were chasing each other, squealing, or playing games in the middle of the street.

"They're staring at us," I said, as I peered out from behind the shawl.

"Of course they are," Annika replied. "We look ridiculous. Him especially." She jabbed a thumb at Crud. "He looks like the Big Bad Wolf dressed up as Grandma."

"Hang on, I think I can fix this." Crud reached into his pocket and pulled out his chopsticks. Shielding the chopsticks with the ends of the shawl, he performed a spell. A moment later, the people who had been staring at us had gone back to whatever they'd been doing.

"Notsen-Glotsen Hex?" I guessed.

It was a spell that Crud was particularly good at, and here in the Nigh, where the Oomphalos was so strong, the spell worked even better than we had hoped. It was as good as an invisibility cloak. People paid us so little attention that we even removed our shawls, and still no one so much as glanced our way.

We made a turn onto Hester Street, where the sidewalks were lined with Folk selling goods—carts piled high with moth-eaten coats and old shoes and stalls with barrels of nuts and candies, oranges and lemons and the little yellow fruits we'd seen in the Piddlebank orchards, which were advertised on the handmade signs as Pinny Fruits.

Most Folk were on foot, but some were riding dogges or in carriages being pulled by dogges, and everyone, it seemed, was in the middle of the street. It was a miracle that no one got smooshed by the carriages that bounced across the cobblestones recklessly fast.

Coming up one of the side streets was a polished black carriage, the spokes of its huge wooden wheels painted yellow. It was drawn by a white dogge, an elegant light-stepping animal with fine curls on its back and feathery fur on its legs. Another carriage, drawn by a much scruffier specimen, was making its way down the main avenue when the two carriages nearly collided. The dogges lunged at each other, teeth bared, rocking the carriages until the drivers managed to calm them down.

The polished black carriage stopped just ahead of us, the driver tugging on the reins so that the dogge lifted its long neck and pranced in place. The driver hopped off his perch and opened the carriage door. Out stepped a man dressed in a green waistcoat and gray trousers, every finger on his hands glittering with rings. He reached back into the carriage and lifted out a small Human boy.

"Caster," Tom said to me before I could ask.

The man set the boy on the ground and, taking his hand, he led him up to a stall selling cheeses. He pointed to a hefty wedge of cheese, which the vender quickly wrapped in brown paper and tied with a string. Then both the vender and the man turned to the little boy. The boy held out his hand and closed his eyes. Little beads of blue light formed in the air above his hand. They hovered for a moment and coagulated, stretched and thinned, squirming like a harassed caterpillar before forming into a disc. The disc dropped heavily into the boy's palm—a small lusterless silver coin. The vender plucked the coin from the boy's hand and dropped it in his apron pocket.

"Wait, did he just cast that money?" I asked.

"Yup. Money, jewelry, buildings," Tom said.

The man hustled the child away from the stall and,

grabbing his hand, led, or really dragged him, down the street.

"So they're basically Human ATMs," said Annika.

"Basically," agreed Tom.

We followed Reynold to the end of the crowded street until I heard Solly's voice in my head, "Here!"

Reynold halted Horst by an open storefront packed with waist-high wooden barrels and an awning that read Pickle Pauli. A man in a stained green apron stood in front of the store, beside a barrel that had been placed on the sidewalk. He stuck his hand straight into the barrel and pulled out a pickle dripping with brine.

"Pickle Pauli's got your extra sours for extra puckers!" he sang out to passersby, crumpling up his face in a clownish way to mimic eating something sour. We were only a few yards in front of him, but he looked right past us. We might as well have been ghosts, with the Notsen-Glotsen Hex in place.

"Put me down please," Solly said to Reynold. He dismounted and carefully scooped Solly out of the sling. I felt an uncomfortable jolt, a wave of her pain as she was placed down on the sidewalk. She walked up to the pickle man, her limp more pronounced.

The hex must have been reserved to the area all around Crud, because as soon as Solly walked away from us, the pickle man noticed her. His animated face grew serious. He shot a quick glance around the street, then hooked his fingers in a gesture to follow him.

"Let's go," Reynold said to us.

We got off our dogges and followed Solly and Pickle Pauli inside the store, which was really just a large stall crammed with barrels of pickles swimming in brine and a wagon loaded with fresh cucumbers.

"You can undo that hex, young man," Solly said to Crud. "Pickle Pauli's a friend."

"I've been hexed?" Pickle Pauli held out his arms and looked down at himself, as though he expected to see feathers sprouting.

"A simple precaution," Solly explained to him. Crud reversed the hex and Pickle Pauli blinked quickly and winced, as if the sun had hurt his eyes. He stared at us in wonder, his eyes passing from one of us to the other. I tensed up as his gaze landed on Tom.

"He's a friend," I said defensively.

"No need to raise your hackles, little lady. Pickle Pauli's no fool." Pickle Pauli grabbed two fresh cucumbers from the wagon. "See these? They both look the same, don't they? Same size, same color. But this one?" He held up the cucumber in his right hand. "Skin's too thick. You can soak it in all the brine you like, it'll make a lousy pickle. Now let me ask you this." He tossed the cucumbers back in the wagon. "If I can tell a good cucumber from a lousy one, you think I can't tell a good Imp from a bad one? Pickle Pauli knows, I tell you, Pickle Pauli knows—"

"Where is it?" Solly interrupted.

"Where is . . . ? Oh right. It's the Wicket you want."

Pickle Pauli squeezed between two barrels and stopped at one off by itself. He slapped its side. "This is it."

"Wait, that's the Wicket?" Annika asked. "A *pickle barrel*?"

"A pickle barrel makes a beautiful Wicket, a perfect Wicket." He slapped the side of the barrel again, more forcefully. "The best."

"Has anyone come through the Wicket today?" Solly asked.

Pickle Pauli shrugged one shoulder. "Not a soul. Been quiet as a tomb."

"Mary should have been here by now," Solly fretted.

"Mary? You mean Mary Car—"

"Shhh!" Solly said.

"Sorry, sorry, I'm used to shouting all day." He lowered his voice. "Well, you can wait here if you like. Help yourself to pickles. Sours are over there, half-sours by the window. Extra sours in the back." He left us to go outside again, shaking his head and muttering, "Mary Carpenter coming through my own pickle barrel? Imagine that."

Reynold followed Pickle Pauli to stand guard outside the store's entrance. Winston hadn't sounded the alarm once since we'd entered the City, but I guess Reynold was taking no chances.

"Well, I don't mind being off that dogge for a while," Annika said, plopping down on the floor. "I'm sore all over."

Solly and I both stood vigil by the Wicket, our eyes on the barrel's opening, watching for Mary. I felt quivery deep in my gut, though I wasn't sure if it was my nerves or Solly's. So much was riding on Mary. If she didn't know where River was, I wasn't sure how we were going to find him.

"I'm starving!" Crud said as he reached into one of the barrels and pulled out a pickle. "Anyone else want one?"

"Give one here," Annika said to Crud.

"Nell?" Crud asked me.

I shook my head. I was too nervous to eat now. Tom waved off the offer too.

"Oh right," Crud said to him. "I forgot that you only eat stuff that rots your teeth."

"I'd give anything for a chocolate bar," Tom said wistfully. "Or some Twizzlers."

"Oh, wait a sec!" I reached into my pocket and pulled out the packet of candy wrapped in newspaper. "I won these on the boat. I don't know if candy from the Nigh is as good as the stuff from the Hither—"

"It's not," said Tom, perking up and taking the packet of candy from me. "But it's better than pickles."

He unfolded the newspaper, revealing a pile of little dark brown pebbles that looked like rabbit droppings, and popped a few into his mouth.

"Anyone else want?" Tom asked.

"I'll try," Crud said, and he took the packet from Tom and plucked up one of the candies, then stopped.

"Nell." His voice sounded odd as he stared down at the candy.

"What?"

"Look."

I walked over to him and looked down at the candy, sitting in its newspaper wrapping. Crud brushed aside some of the candy to reveal a notice in the paper: Owner of the Golden Imaginarium, fined for loitering in Delaney Court on East Ninth Street and operating without a license.

"The Golden Imaginarium." I looked up at Crud.

"So I guess it's not a video game after all."

30

TENTACLES

"What are you guys talking about?" Annika asked.

I reached into my pocket and pulled out the scrap of paper torn from River's poster.

Tom and Annika read the note over my shoulder. Even Solly had limped over to my side to have a look at it.

"Where did you get that?" she asked sharply.

"I found it yesterday, back home. I thought it might have something to do with my brother."

"That's Mary's handwriting."

"Mary? Are you sure?" I asked.

"Certainly I'm sure," she replied.

"So what does it mean? Why would she leave the message for me?"

"I don't think she *did* leave it for you. I think she left it for herself."

"I don't understand."

"She wrote notes like that to help her to remember. When Mary is here, in the Nigh, she's quick and clever and can outthink most everyone. But in the Hither, well . . . she struggles. She becomes confused. Her memory fails her. It's from traveling between the two worlds so often and for many, many years. So when she's in the Hither, she has to write notes to herself—important things that she needs to remember—and she leaves the notes in places where she'll be sure to see them. That's what I think this is. A note to herself."

There was a whispery whoosh of wind from the back of the store. We all turned in time to see what looked like an electrical cord flick out from behind one of the pickle barrels. It snapped at the air, then disappeared behind the barrel again.

"What was that?" Annika jumped to her feet and weaved between the cluster of barrels toward the back of the store.

"Um, you all might want to have a look at this," she said.

We made our way over to her and found, hunched against the back wall, a tarry black creature about the size of a fire hydrant covered with feelers. One by one, the feelers lifted and unfurled, the tips quivering.

"What is that thing?" I whispered.

It must have heard me because its feelers suddenly slapped at the ground and the creature rose up to its full height. This was no fire hydrant. It was seven feet tall at least. The skin on its body was blistered and appeared to be covered with a sticky black substance while its face was eerily normal. It was the face of any number of guys that you might see in a vegan doughnut shop—neatly trimmed beard, hair brushed back off his forehead, and wearing a pair of sunglasses. Most chilling of all, he was smiling.

Crud let out a curse word. The creature's smile turned into an O of shock. One of its feelers whipped through the air and came down on a pickle barrel, slicing it cleanly in half. Pickles and pickle juice spilled across the floor.

I felt something wrap around my waist and I screamed, but it was only Tom, pulling me backward, just as another feeler lashed the air so close to me that I could hear it crack.

"Go, go, go!" Annika cried.

Crud scooped up Solly and we ran, our shoes splashing through the pickle juice, as the creature continued to slash at the barrels, scudding between them until it left the store and was out on the street.

Folk screamed and scattered as the creature slashed at the pavement, gouging out cobblestones and flinging them in the air. Its razor-sharp feelers ripped through carts of food and clothes and candy in a mad frenzy, slicing fruit and lacerating hats, and through it all the creature's face continued to grin pleasantly. It was only a matter of seconds before those feelers were going to come down on one of the Folk.

I reached into my jacket and pulled out my chopsticks. This time I wouldn't hesitate to perform the Miten-Ei Spell. The creature had turned its back to me as I pressed my wrists together, ready to perform the spell. In a flash, the creature whipped around to face me, its rictus grin plastered on its face, more terrifying somehow than its slashing feelers. The next instant, I was slammed to the ground, striking the pavement painfully, before I was dragged like a sack across the cobblestones. If the creature had sliced off any of my limbs, I couldn't feel it yet—I'd heard that could sometimes happen when you're in shock—and I tried to scramble to my feet even as I was being dragged, stumbling and flopping, until finally I was released. I got to my feet, chopsticks at the ready, and found Wallace standing beside me, his tail wagging tentatively. It took me a second to realize what had happened. Wallace must have rushed in and dragged me away from the beast.

"What were you thinking?" Tom ran up to me, with Crud and Annika close behind.

"You'd be in a hundred little pieces right now if it weren't for that dogge," Annika said.

There was a tremendous crash across the street as the creature's feelers came down on the polished black carriage parked outside the cheese stall. It split the carriage in two, causing the terrified dogge that had been pulling it to gallop off with the front half of the carriage wobbling helplessly behind him.

I raised my chopsticks once again, pressing my wrists together.

"Don't!" Tom had wrapped a hand around my chopsticks. "The last time you did the spell, the Magician appeared right after. I think it signals them somehow."

"Well, we can't just let that thing kill everyone!"

"I've got this," Annika said. She whipped out her chopsticks and started a spell.

"Smart, Annika, smart!" Crud said approvingly, having obviously recognized it.

"What is she doing?" I asked.

"It basically causes instant karma. Watch."

It never failed to amaze me how much more powerful our spells were in the Nigh. The Oomphalos was like a massive signal boost. Annika's spell sparked and crackled in the air, bursts within bursts of light, like tiny fireworks. The creature saw it and turned to us, his grin still in place. He lifted a feeler, then another and another. Oh yeah, he was gearing up to slice and dice.

"Hurry, Annika," I pleaded as she kept forming her spell.

At that moment, the carriage's owner—the man with the Human boy—emerged from a store just up the street, cradling his parcels in one hand and gripping the little boy's wrist in the other. When he saw the demolished remnant of his carriage, he bellowed in outrage. The monster turned to look at him and that's when the man saw the creature. The man's mouth was open in midbellow, but no sound came out now. The little boy pulled back, trying to get away, but the man was frozen in place with terror.

I watched the creature's spine bend back, readying itself for a fresh assault.

Annika lifted her hand and spooled the lights from her spell around her pointer finger. With a quick jerk of her arm, she flung the lights at the creature, hitting it square on the back of its head. The monster howled and whipped around. His feelers lashed out toward us, but before they could reach us, they took a sharp U-turn and sliced at each other, lopping off several feelers. The amputated feelers fell to the ground and twitched for a few seconds before growing still. The creature wailed; whether from pain or frustration, it was hard to tell. He raised a half dozen more feelers and whipped them through the air at us, but these too turned and sliced at themselves. Again and again the creature tried to attack, and each time it wound up attacking itself, until all that was left were a few stunted and useless limbs attached to the tarry black body, which was already weaving around unsteadily. Its face still wore a grin but its legs buckled, and then the creature crumpled completely and collapsed on the street.

For a moment we all stared at it. In movies, monsters always have a second wind. That's just one more reason I hate horror flicks. Reynold, though, had probably never seen a movie in his life. He walked right up to the creature before we could stop him and knelt down beside it.

"Dead," he confirmed after a moment.

"Is it really though?" Annika asked.

Reynold poked it and we all cringed, waiting for one of those tentacles to suddenly grow back and lash out. "Oh yeah," Reynold said. "Totally dead."

The little boy was sobbing in high-pitched gasps as the man examined the remains of his carriage. I saw the opportunity and took it. Running up, I grabbed the boy's hand, but the man caught me.

"Hoi! What are you doing?" he cried, rushing over and pinching the boy's upper arm in his bejeweled fingers. "He's mine!"

"You bought him," I snapped back. "You bought him like you bought your cheese."

"That's right." He tipped his chin up, the residue of the recent fear already beginning to melt back into smugness. "I bought him, so I own him."

I considered what sort of spell I could use on him. Maybe I could animate his cheese, although I wasn't sure what cheese would do when it was animated. I was scrolling through the scanty choices of spells that I had in my magical playbook when Crud lumbered up to us and, with one quick jab, punched the man in the nose. The man stumbled and fell backward. Crud scooped the boy up under his arm like a football, and stalked off.

Which just goes to show you, sometimes it's best not to overthink things.

31

THE GOLDEN IMAGINARIUM

The entire street was in shambles. We had stolen a boy. Well, restolen him, to be fair, but still. We had not exactly kept a low profile.

Crud, Annika, Tom, and I stood on the street and watched as Pickle Pauli inspected the carnage in his shop. The poor guy was crying. Every pickle barrel had been destroyed, including the Wicket.

An ugly suspicion crept into my mind. This was the third time a creature had appeared near a Wicket—once when Vanessa came through, then again when Solly was attacked, and now. What if these monsters were guarding the Wickets? What if the Magicians had put them there to prevent Mary from coming back to the Nigh, or to destroy her, whichever came first?

My heart sank at this thought, for Mary's sake, and for River's.

"You guys, she's not looking good," Annika said, nodding toward Solly.

Solly was sitting back on her haunches, the little boy by

her side, watching Reynold adjust the dogges' saddles. Her wound looked worse than ever. The stitches had popped in the middle and the whole thing looked red and mottled. Her breath was labored too—I could see her rib cage rise and fall quickly beneath her gray fur.

"Next Wicket to open is the one at Bethesda Fountain," Reynold said as he buckled Wallace's cinch, then let down the stirrups. "So that's where we're headed next."

I knew that Wicket. In fact, the first time I'd ever been in the Nigh, I had come through the Wicket in Bethesda Fountain. Of course, I had seen the very same fountain back home too. In the Hither, people came from all over the world to see the huge bronze angel that stood on a pedestal, high above the fountain in Central Park. In the Nigh, though, the angel wasn't simply a statue. In the Nigh, the angel Bethesda was very much alive, as were the three giant toddlers that stood on the pedestal below hers—the Holy Terrors, as she called them.

"It's risky," Reynold continued. "The Magicians keep a close eye on that Wicket, but Bethesda is tough as nails and she's on our side. She'll sneak Mary through if she can." He slapped Wallace's saddle. "He's ready for you two."

The four of us exchanged looks as Reynold began to work on Bluebell's saddle. We all realized what we needed to do. It was Tom who said it: "We're going on without you, Reynold."

"No, you're not. Too dangerous." Reynold didn't even look at us as he unbuckled Bluebell's loose cinch.

"We're not exactly helpless," Annika said. "Do I have to remind you that we were the ones who took down that creature?"

"And we have the Notsen-Glotsen Hex to keep us hidden," Crud added.

"I said no." Reynold pulled Bluebell's cinch so tightly that she turned and growled at him.

"Solly can't keep going. Look at her," I urged him quietly. "She's in rough shape."

Reynold's eyes cut over to Solly, but he said nothing.

"What would your sister want you to do?" I asked.

It was a cheap shot, but it worked. I saw his throat tick with a hard swallow. In the end we convinced him to take Solly and the little boy back to Piddlebank. It was really the only logical thing to do. Convincing Solly, though, was another story. She straight-up refused. It was Annika who persuaded her.

"I'm going to tell you what my track coach said to me when I sprained my ankle last year and wanted to keep running," Annika said to Solly. "My coach said, 'Don't be a big dummy, Rapp. Rest up. Get better. You have plenty of time to be a hero in the future.'"

We headed north in silence. I think it finally hit us that we were now well and truly alone, with only some spotty magical skills and the Notsen-Glotsen Hex to keep us hidden. Although we almost didn't need the hex since hardly anyone was out on the streets. Word about the creature must have spread fast.

I was beginning to recognize things that had been cast by children. They were always slightly off. The front doors were too tall or the bricks were too large, created as they were from the perspective of a child's imperfect memory.

We were halfway down Ninth Street when a brightly painted wooden caravan pulled by a pair of ancient-looking dogges came out of a courtyard. Wallace lurched sideways to avoid it, slamming into Bluebell, who bared her teeth and snapped at him. To add to the insult, the caravan driver gave us the finger before she snapped the reins and her dogges took off down the street, the caravan rattling behind them.

"Jerk!" Annika yelled at her while I patted Wallace's neck to console him. But Crud reached back and slapped Bluebell's side. "Go!" he shouted.

Bluebell took off running, with Tom nearly flung backward before grabbing on to Crud's waist.

"What's he doing?" I asked.

"Road rage," Annika said.

I urged Wallace to follow just as Crud had overtaken the caravan and yanked Bluebell's reins to the right, cutting off the caravan.

The woman had pulled back on her own dogges' reins so sharply that the whole front of her caravan lifted slightly off the ground before it slammed back down. The dogges, gray-muzzled and fat-bellied, whined in protest.

"What do you think you're doing?" the woman yelled from the driver's perch as she tried to settle her dogges. "If you don't have any control over those big dumb brutes, stay off the road!"

But Crud wasn't paying any attention to her. In fact, he looked as far from rage as possible. He was grinning from ear to ear. Tom was looking pretty happy too, gesturing wildly for us to come over.

The caravan itself was a work of art, shaped like a giant tube set on large spoked wooden wheels. It was painted sun-gold with pale green vines trellising up the corners. Carved painted birds and insects framed the narrow back door and meandered around a large shuttered window.

And then I saw it.

There was a sign nailed to the side of the caravan with words painted in swirly blue letters: THE GOLDEN IMAGINARIUM.

I looked at Crud. He smiled and held out his hands, palms up. "Ta-da!"

32

TILDA

We dismounted and walked up to the woman. She wore a black watch cap rolled up on the edges so it looked like she had a cereal bowl on her head, with reddish-gold hair spilling out from under it. She was a pretty woman with a broad, freckled face and the wide-set eyes that so many Folk had. Those eyes quickly went from anger to astonishment.

"Humans!"

"We needed to talk to you—" I started to say.

"Get inside!" she said, glancing up and down the street. "Door's around back. Quick, quick, before you're seen."

We walked around to the back of the caravan and Crud and Annika went inside. Before I could follow them, though, Tom grabbed my elbow.

"Wait."

"Why?"

"I don't know. I'm not sure about this." Tom glanced at the caravan warily. In the past I'd noticed that his eyes often shifted colors as quickly as the ocean. Now his eyes were a dark, troubled gray.

"The note was in Mary's handwriting," I reminded him. "That means Mary thought this was important for some reason. And look." I gave my right braid a slight jiggle and smiled. "Not a peep from Winston."

The caravan's door opened and Annika popped her head out. "Are you guys coming or not?"

I turned to Tom. "Four of us, one of her, right?"

He nodded but he didn't look convinced.

It was a tight squeeze, but we all managed to fit. The inside of the caravan was as colorful as the outside, with layers of little carpets swirling with colors. Dangling above our heads were dozens and dozens of wooden marionette puppets hanging from hooks in the ceiling—a pale blond princess in a white gown and a bearded woodcutter; dragons and skeletons; green cats and purple dogges, and every sort of bird imaginable. A wooden worktable built into the wall was strewn with puppet heads and limbs, chisels and metal hand files, paints and brushes, and wires looped around a pegboard. A dozen fully costumed puppets were hung on a narrow strip of wood behind a red velvet curtain that spanned the inside of the shuttered window.

The woman, dressed as she was in a black turtleneck sweater, black canvas pants, and the black watch cap, looked like a cat burglar. She put her hands on her hips and stared at us in disbelief.

"Are Humans really this stupid? You're lucky the Magicians haven't snatched you already. What are you thinking?"

"We were careful," Crud said. "I cast a spell so that we wouldn't be noticed."

"The Notsen-Glotsen?"

Crud nodded.

"Well, guess what? The Notsen-Glotsen Hex doesn't work on Magicians," she said.

"It doesn't?" Crud asked.

"No, it doesn't." The woman sat down on a small cot and folded her arms. "Who are you?"

We told her our names.

"I'm Tilda, owner of the Golden Imaginarium, the only traveling puppet show in the Nigh. Well, as far as I know it is. So." She looked at me. "You said you had something to talk to me about."

I fished out the scrap of paper from my pocket and handed it to her.

She read it, then shrugged. "So?"

"So Mary Carpenter wrote it."

"Mary Carpenter?" She looked back down at the note. "That's strange. Mary Carpenter came to see me a couple of weeks ago."

"Do you know her?" Crud asked.

"Never met her before. She just showed up at one of my shows. She came inside the caravan afterward."

"Why?"

Tilda leaned forward, elbows on her knees, and inspected us all for a moment.

"Magicians from the Hither, huh?" She took off her watch cap and ran her fingers through her hair. "It's been a long time since I've seen some good magic. Go on. Do something for me."

"But why would Mary—?" I started, but she interrupted. She held up a finger. "Magic first."

"They're much better at magic than I am," I said, nodding toward Crud and Annika.

But Tilda ignored that. "You." She nodded at me. "Do something pretty."

She placed the tips of her fingers together in anticipation. Well, she was going to be royally disappointed. I only had a few simple tricks up my sleeve—except for one that apparently killed things. I was most comfortable with animation spells, despite their tendency to spin out of control.

I looked around the caravan for something to animate. Hanging by its strings behind the stage was a pink flamingo puppet made of painted wood with long silvery legs and a curved black-tipped beak. Good enough.

I took out my chopsticks and began the Oifen Shoifen Spell. I felt the Oomphalos energy gathering, making the air around my hands pop and fizz against my skin. The flamingo's body softened and the flat pink of its painted skin grew lofty and soft with actual feathers. Its eyes blinked and its long neck lifted, like a snake rearing up. It struggled to its feet, but stumbled, finding itself tethered to the marionette strings. With a hoarse angry squawk, it twisted its neck around, clamped its beak on one of the strings, and snapped it in two. One by one, it bit down on its strings until it freed itself completely.

"Here we go, get ready for the chaos," Annika muttered.

I glanced over at Tilda to see if she was annoyed, but she was watching the bird with interest.

When it was finally free, the flamingo hopped off the stage and onto the floor. It was only about the size of a small chicken, but in every other respect it was all flamingo. Its delicate legs, as thin as my chopsticks, tested each step as it walked around the room. It stretched its neck up, puffed out its chest, and spread its wings, flapping them.

"Not bad." Tilda smiled.

The flamingo approached her with that odd tiptoeing flamingo walk. Tilda bent down to stroke its head, and the bird pulled its neck back and jabbed its beak into her shin.

"Ow!"

I tried to reverse the spell, but it didn't take. The bird hopped to one side, then lunged in for another jab, this time at Tilda's ankle.

"Nell's a little shaky on the cease-and-desist part," Annika remarked coolly.

I shot her a dirty look and tried again. The bird paused for a moment, turning its head this way and that as though listening for something. Then it let out a squawk and took a running leap at Tilda, launching itself at her face. Tilda drew back quickly, holding up her hands to ward off the bird.

That's when I saw it.

"Nell!" Tom hissed. He had seen it too.

"Chopsticks out!" I cried.

Annika and Crud pulled out their chopsticks instantly. No questions asked. That really impressed me.

"She's a Magician," I told them.

"How do you know?" Crud asked.

"She has a triple life line on her hand."

"Is that a thing?" Annika asked.

"It is a thing."

"I wondered why the Notsen-Glotsen Hex didn't work on her," Crud said.

Oh. Right. That too.

The flamingo made a prolonged squawk that ended abruptly. The bird stumbled and fell. One long leg kicked out, as if in protest, and then the bird lay still. Its eyes flattened to black paint and its wings settled against its wooden torso. The spell had ended.

33

THE FENNICK

Tilda held her hands up in surrender as we trained our chopsticks on her.

"I don't understand," I said to her. "Why would Mary Carpenter want to talk to you? It makes no sense. You're a Magician. You're one of them."

"*Was* a Magician," Tilda said. "And she came to see this."

She lowered one hand, but Annika barked at her, "Hands in the air!"

She lifted her hand again. "You do it then," she said to me. "Pull down the collar of my sweater."

I glanced over at the others. They were laser-focused on her, their chopsticks practically vibrating with the threat of a spell. I cautiously approached her, then reached out and pulled down the neck of her sweater. Stretching from under her clavicle all the way up to her right ear was a long sickle-shaped scar. Tiny stitch marks ticked the edges so that it looked like a silver centipede on her skin.

"You're a Fennick!" Tom said with wonder in his voice.

"A what?" I asked, releasing the neck of her sweater.

"A Fennick," Tom said. "Her magic was removed. That's what the scar is from. It's a punishment for something." He turned to her. "What did you do?"

Tilda leveled her gaze at us but said nothing.

"Look, we're all delinquents here," Annika said. "Crud tried to strangle his science teacher, Tom's a . . . well, he's an Imp, so there's that. Nell has a gambling addiction—"

"Not really a—" I started to defend myself.

"And me?" Annika continued. "Well, I was wrongfully accused, but I'm not perfect."

I snorted.

"So? What did you do?" Annika repeated Tom's question.

Tilda took a breath, then said, "I killed twelve people."

We had all lowered our chopsticks, but you'd better believe that we raised them again now.

"It was a very long time ago," she said hurriedly. "I was a child when it happened."

"When what happened?" I asked.

"There was a bridge. It was built between the City and Brooklyn. A Human girl had casted it, and I destroyed it."

"That was you?" I asked.

She nodded. "My father was a Magician who worked for the Minister. I went to see the bridge's opening ceremony. I was watching from the banks of the river, along with my cousins. I remember seeing the girl who had made the bridge. It was the first time I'd ever seen a Human. She was older than me by a few years. They had dressed her up like a princess in a long white gown, threaded jewels through her hair, and paraded her in front of everyone. She looked miserable. I felt so sorry for her, though I wouldn't have admitted it out loud. My cousins already thought I was strange because my mother was Folk, but my heart hurt for that girl. I knew what Magicians did with the Human children. It wasn't right. I couldn't imagine being taken away from my parents like that.

"Anyway, my cousins and I were playing. I was the youngest, and they were all good at magic, much better than I was. They said it was because I was only half Magician, that I'd never be any good at it. They were showing off. Doing spells that made pebbles grow wings and flutter around like butterflies. They could make their eyes turn colors—orange to pink to stripes. I couldn't do any of that stuff. I'd only learned to do the simplest things, and I hardly ever got them right anyway. So I told them I had a special spell that no one had ever seen before. I didn't, of course, and they knew it and made fun of me. So I pretended. I started to move my hands like they did, and I actually could feel the magic building around me. I almost stopped because it scared me, but I knew my cousins would think I was lying, so I kept going."

Tilda's hand went to her neck, her finger rubbing the scar beside her ear.

"I heard the screams first. And then I saw the bridge just . . . just crumpling. My father and that Human girl, they all just . . ." Her voice broke and she shook her head.

Something occurred to me then. Something I had

missed. I felt an electric buzzing in my chest. A sense that the pieces were coming together, beginning to make sense.

"Afterward, the Magicians took my magic from me," Tilda continued. "I was lucky that was all they did, but my mother pleaded with them. She said I was too young to know what I was doing. They spared my life, but everyone knew what I'd done, and either they were afraid of me or they made fun of me for being a Fennick. As soon as I was old enough, I left home and started to roam. I went places where no one would know who I was. I'd stay for a while and then I was on the road again, always moving. One day I ran into a traveling puppeteer. A kind old man, who hired me on, taught me how to build marionette puppets and how to work them. I was good at it—I built all of these puppets. Just before he died, he gave me this caravan. So here I am. Still roaming."

"It was eleven people," I said.

"What?"

"Eleven people died that day, not twelve," I insisted. "The girl who casted the bridge lived."

Everyone looked at me, baffled, but I was sure I was right.

"How do you know that?" Crud asked.

"Because Solly showed us her memory of it. Remember? It was like a film playing in our minds because Solly was there. We were seeing it through Solly's eyes. Right before the bridge broke, that girl smiled. In our minds, it looked like she was smiling right at us. That's because she was smiling at Solly. Solly said she'd known Mary since Mary was a child. It was Mary who casted that bridge. It was Mary who fell in the river. But she survived."

"Then she must have known who I was," Tilda realized. "When Mary came to see me and asked to see the scar, she knew who I was. She knew what I had done."

"Did she say anything to you?" Crud asked.

Tilda shook her head. "She looked at the scar, then left."

We were all silent for a moment.

"Listen" Crud said, "if we're going to make it to the next open Wicket, we need to get going."

"Right," I said, and we started for the door, but Tilda stopped us.

"Wait. Which Wicket?" she asked.

"The one at Bethesda Fountain."

"I'll take you in the caravan," Tilda said. "It will be safer that way."

"How fast are your dogges?" Crud asked.

"Not very."

"Okay, then our dogges can pull the caravan," Crud said.

"Do they know how?" Tilda asked.

"I guess we'll find out."

34

ℬETHESDA

After Tilda unhitched her own dogges and led them back to the courtyard she'd emerged from, she hitched up Bluebell and Wallace to the caravan.

As it turned out, the two of them did not know how to pull a caravan. They were fast learners, however, and after some hairy false starts where one of them would pull straight while the other one would turn to the left or right, they sorted themselves out.

The caravan raced uptown. It was a rocky ride, especially over the cobbled streets. The wooden puppets clattered over our heads, their legs dancing wild jigs as they threatened to come down on us at any second. Tilda took the turns at top speed, tossing us into each other while the tools from her workbench were flung all over the caravan and occasionally at our heads.

"If she ever decides to move to the Hither, she'd make a great cabdriver," Crud said.

The rattling of the caravan wheels suddenly subsided. I looked out of the tiny slit between the wooden shutters covering the puppet stage window. We were in Central Park now. I could see the trees flying past as the caravan sped toward Bethesda Terrace, where the angel Bethesda presided over her Wicket in the fountain.

The caravan slowed. We had arrived. And then, to my dismay, I heard it:

"*Wickle-wickle-feee! Wickle-wickle-feee!*"

As if to confirm Winston's warning, there was a tremendous crash from outside the caravan and I heard Wallace's yelping, panicked bark.

"I think we may be too late," we heard Tilda call from her perch on the driver's platform.

All of us piled out the back door—I'm embarrassed to say that I forgot about the high step and tumbled rather than stepped out, but never mind—and we all gazed around the plaza in silent shock.

Deep canals had been gouged into the plaza's brick pavement, radiating from the tree line flanking the plaza and winding toward the fountain. Trees had been uprooted and were lying on their sides while stray bricks had been flung everywhere. To my relief, the fountain was still standing with the bronze angel Bethesda on the top pedestal. But her wings were folded around herself and she was oddly still, which is a weird thing to say about a statue, I know, but not about a statue in the Nigh. The pedestal below, on which the three giant toddlers usually stood, was empty. The Holy Terrors were gone.

Whatever had done this was nowhere in sight. The whole place was still and quiet. Too quiet.

"Where are you, monster?" Crud whispered.

"Maybe it's come and gone," Annika suggested.

"I don't think so," I whispered. "Winston sounded the alarm."

"Shh!" Tom said. "Listen."

There was a burbling sound, like water boiling. It grew louder and faster and then the water in the fountain erupted, as though someone had detonated a bomb inside it. The chisel-shaped head of a massive snake, big around as a truck tire, shot up out of the water. Its skin was the shifting colors of an oil spill, and circling the top of the snake's skull, like a crown, was a ring of nubbly cartilage. The snake weaved its body higher and higher in the air, until it reached the hem of Bethesda's dress.

"Girl has some inches on her," Bethesda said, staring at the creature.

As soon as the snake began to slither onto Bethesda's pedestal, Bethesda pulled back her bare foot and gave the creature a swift kick.

Bethesda is no lightweight and her foot is the size of a two-by-four, but the snake hardly seemed to register the blow. It flicked its black tongue out of its mouth, the forked tip quivering. On top of its head, one of the prongs on "the crown" began to uncoil, and a new snake appeared. This one was quick and supple, and it darted between Bethesda's feet before she could stop it. Bethesda shifted to the side to stomp on it, and when she did, I spied one of the Holy Terrors peering out from beneath her wings— a huge, bronze-colored toddler. One by one, other snakes were uncoiling from the great snake's crown, each one of them sliding onto the pedestal. Bethesda fought them off, but she was so overwhelmed that several of the snakes had managed to coil themselves around one of the Holy Terrors' chubby legs and drag him out from his hiding place.

"You touch my babies and I will smack you to the moon!" Bethesda screamed, swatting at the snake heads as they dodged her blows and wrapped themselves around another Holy Terror.

I pulled out my chopsticks, but Tom grabbed my wrist. "You can't!"

"I have to! Look what that thing is doing!"

"I'm going to try something." Crud lifted his chopsticks and his spell fairly exploded out of them, looking like an army of manic fireflies charging the fountain.

"A binding spell?" Annika looked at Crud doubtfully as the sparks hit the snake, then turned liquid and spread across its body in a crisscross of filaments. "Won't it just—?" The snake thrashed wildly until the filaments snapped one by one. "Yeah, do that."

After that, Annika and Crud tossed spells at the creature so fast that the Oomphalos sizzled and crackled in the air, creating a vaporous green afterglow like a fireworks finale, but nothing seemed to faze the creature. The smaller snakes had managed to ensnare all three of the

Holy Terrors now, and though Bethesda had wrapped her mighty arms around the toddlers, they were slowly slipping out of her grasp. One of the Holy Terrors was torn from her arms but managed to grab her ankle as he was pulled down and was now holding on desperately.

Suddenly, the snakes grew still. Their black tongues flicked at the air. They seemed to be listening. One by one, the smaller snakes unraveled themselves from the toddlers and coiled themselves up again on the great snake's skull. The Holy Terror who had been dragged from Bethesda now clambered back up to her and hid beneath her wings with the other two.

The monstrous snake weaved in the air for a moment, then wound itself lower and lower until it was fully submerged in the fountain's water.

"What did you do?" I asked Crud and Annika.

They shook their heads, looking baffled.

"Maybe it just gave up?" Crud said.

"Hmm. Doesn't seem the type," Annika said.

The fountain water started churning with abrupt violence, burbling and splashing, as though a mighty struggle was happening below the surface.

"The Wicket!" I exclaimed. "Someone's coming through the Wicket!"

35

Six Flags

We all ran toward the fountain, and just as we reached its stone rim, something surfaced. It was hard to tell what it was exactly, since it was completely enveloped within the snake's massive coils. Still, just above the uppermost coil, I could make out a pair of braids, each one dyed acid green on the ends.

"It's Vanessa!" I shouted.

Tom charged into the fountain and threw himself on the snake. He slid his arm around the snake's head, just below its jaw, and squeezed, his face reddening with the effort. I saw the snake's coils begin to slacken, and Vanessa pulled one of her arms loose. But a second later, the snake's crown disgorged the other snakes, and they fell on Tom in an instant, wrapping themselves like nooses around his neck.

I had no choice. There was nothing left to do.

I worked the spell as quickly as I could, forcing myself to focus my mind on the creature even as I heard Tom gasping for air. There was a flash of light so bright that I squeezed my eyes shut. When I opened them again, the great snake and its crown of smaller snakes had stopped moving. I could still hear Tom's rasping struggle to breathe, and I ran to the fountain and climbed in, splashing toward the frozen creature. With my thumb and pointer finger, I flicked the great snake on the side of its head. The snake's prisma-colored skin paled, then turned gray. Layer by layer, the skin peeled off the creature's body and crumbled to ash that fell into the water.

"Well, look at that!" Bethesda planted her massive arms on her hips as the Holy Terrors climbed down to the lower pedestal to watch the spectacle.

Vanessa and Tom were caked with ash, and Tom had doubled over, trying to catch his breath.

"All right?" I asked him.

He glanced up at me and nodded. Though his face was still red, he was grinning.

Bethesda stepped off her pedestal and into the fountain, her feet displacing so much water that it sloshed over the fountain's rim. She scooped out the wet piles of ash from the water and deposited them on the ground, muttering, "Nasty thing, sludging up my fountain. Now tell me, baby," she said to me. "How on earth did you do that?"

"Miten-Ei Spell," Vanessa answered for me. "Never seen it done before. Impressive!" She looked around the plaza and took in all the destruction. "Your brother's no slouch either."

"What do you mean?" I asked.

"It's him, Nell. He's the one casting these creatures."

"River? No. That can't be true!"

"Pretty sure it is. We figured it out not too long ago. One of our people spotted some intense casting lights coming from a place they shouldn't be coming from. The only kid we know that could have produced such powerful casting lights is River."

I remembered the tiny beads of light that the little boy had formed when he casted the coin. I could only imagine what sort of lights casting that monster snake would have produced.

"But why would he do it?" I asked.

"My guess is he's trying to seal off the Nigh from the Hither. Destroy the Wickets. Without them, the Magicians can't take any more kids."

"But he's destroying more than the Wickets. He's putting lives in danger."

"I know that, but it's an act of desperation, Nell. It's the act of someone who feels they're all out of options."

"*Wickle-wickle-feee! Wickle-wickle-feee!*"

Winston sounded the alarm a moment before Tilda called out to us. She pointed to a line of black specks that were rising up in the sky from the center of the City, like a reverse tornado. Magicians. "Hurry!" she cried. "Get in the caravan!"

"Nope, a caravan won't work," Vanessa said as she waded out of the fountain. "We're going over water."

"Over water? Why?" I asked.

"Because that's where River is." She turned to Bethesda. "Those wings aren't just for show, are they?"

In answer, Bethesda rolled her massive shoulders and her wings unfolded, fanning out behind her. They were awesome to behold, muscular and supple, their rust-colored feathers rippling as she extended them to their full length. They flapped a few times and she rose up out of the fountain, water dripping from her toes.

"Sweet!" Vanessa said as Bethesda folded her wings against her back and descended again. "How many of us can you take?"

"Well, I may be big, honey, but I'm not a bus," Bethesda replied. "I can take two. The Holy Terrors can take the rest."

She beckoned to the giant toddlers who had been watching from their perch on the statue's lower pedestal. Now the three of them eagerly jumped down and splashed into the fountain. On closer inspection, I could see they had wings too, flattened against their backs like empty knapsacks.

For the record, I'm terrified of heights. When my class went on a field trip to Six Flags, they had to stop the Ferris wheel to get me off because I had puked on the kid next to me. I sat on a bench with the room parent for the rest of the time. But River was somewhere over the water, and we were not going to get there by caravan. So I sucked it up, grabbed onto the edge of Bethesda's wing for balance, and climbed on her back.

"Put your arms around my neck," Bethesda told me.

I lay down on my stomach between her wings, and reached around her neck.

"Tighter," Bethesda said.

"I won't hurt you, will I?" I asked.

"With your noodle arms? Honey, stop."

So I wrapped my arms tightly around her neck, clasping them at the front of her throat.

"Now you, pretty boy," she said to Tom.

Tom swung himself onto her back easily. I shifted over for him so he could grab onto her neck, but instead he sat back, legs stretched out as if he were settling into a lawn chair.

"Aren't you going to hold on?" I asked nervously.

"If Bluebell wasn't able to dump me, I'm pretty sure I can stay on an angel's back."

"Show off," I muttered.

"That leaves one for each of you," Bethesda said to the Holy Terrors.

The giant toddlers each made a beeline for Annika, which led to a tussle with lots of kicking and elbow jabbing until one of them managed to grab Annika's hand and held it up like a trophy.

"Good boy," Bethesda told him. "Now pick her up. Carefully. She's made of bones, not bronze."

The toddler picked up Annika and cradled her like a baby.

"Fine. Whatever," Annika said resignedly. "Just don't drop me."

There was another scramble, this time for Vanessa, leaving Crud as the booby prize. To be fair, Crud was a heavy load, even for a giant baby.

"I'll take good care of the dogges until you get back," Tilda said.

When we were all sorted, Bethesda spread her wings. As soon as we began to rise, I felt my stomach flip-flop and I groaned. I had a feeling it was going to be Six Flags all over again, except this time I wasn't getting off the ride.

36

The Flight

I know Bethesda must have been trying to keep herself steady, but as we rose higher and higher, the muscles of her back buckled and shifted, and my body rolled with each movement. I squeezed my eyes shut and pressed my face against Bethesda's neck, which was cool but alive with tiny movements as she flew.

"All right?" Tom asked.

"Yes. No," I replied.

I dreaded the thought of puking in front of Tom even more than the fact that we were in the air.

"I won't let you fall, Nell."

"Famous last words."

He laughed. "We're not really that high up. Open your eyes."

I squinted one eye open and looked over Bethesda's shoulder. Tom was right. She was only a few yards above the tallest trees in the park. We passed over the park's heavy stone wall and out into the streets, where we flew perilously close to the buildings. I could see straight into the windows of some of them, locking eyes with a few shocked Folk.

I turned around to see where the others were. The Holy Terrors were airborne, but that's the best I could say for them. They seemed to fly as unpredictably as paper airplanes, zigzagging, zooming up and dipping low above the heads of startled Folk. Annika was barking orders at her toddler who, grinning wildly, was making a game of dropping down and knocking hats off Folks' heads, while Vanessa's Holy Terror seemed to be drifting aimlessly from left to right.

"When we get to the river," Vanessa called up to Bethesda, "turn south."

Bethesda banked to the left, her body angling so sharply that I felt myself sliding, but Tom grabbed my waist and held me steady until she leveled out again. The river was below us now. We could see the great ships crowding the harbor, their masts rising so high in the air that Tom actually reached down and touched one of them.

I turned around to see where the others were and spotted the dark squadron of Magicians passing over the City in the distance, an awkwardly flying army of a few dozen at least.

Annika's Holy Terror was lagging far behind, while Vanessa's was flying off course, heading closer to New Jersey. What was worse, it looked like Crud's Holy Terror was tiring. His wings seemed to be straining and he was losing altitude. At one point, he dropped down so low that his huge foot trailed in the water before he lifted himself up again. But a few moments later, I heard a mighty splash and looked down to see Crud's Holy Terror in the river, his arms frantically thrashing, while Crud was clinging to his neck.

"Bethesda!"

"I see it, honey! Hang on!" Bethesda turned so sharply that Tom flung himself on his stomach, one arm tight over my back, pinning us down as she dove toward the river.

If you've ever wondered whether a bronze statue can float in water, the answer is no, it cannot. The Holy Terror sunk like a stone. Or a chunk of bronze. Crud was still above water, treading, thank goodness, but I doubted he was much of a swimmer himself.

I caught a glint of metal beneath the water, just a flash.

"There!" I called to Bethesda, who shifted to where I was pointing and plunged her hand in the river. She felt beneath the waves as her wings flapped double time to keep herself aloft, but when she pulled her hand out of the water, it was empty.

I looked for the glint of metal again, when to my horror, Crud went under the water too.

"Tom!"

"I know! I'm going in!" He started to get up but the next moment, Crud's head reappeared and he called up, "Here! Here!" pointing down at the water in front of him.

Bethesda rose up and dove down again, then thrust her arm in the river. She pulled back and this time there was resistance. The next moment, she was gripping a chubby bronze hand with dimpled knuckles. She pulled the toddler up, her wings pumping, struggling against his weight.

There was a flash in the air above us, and I looked up to see a Magician. He must have been more adept at flying than the others because he had broken ranks from the rest, who were far behind him. He was a flashy dresser for a Magician, with a bright orange shirt splashed with blue begonias, straining across a potbelly. His hands were shaping a spell. And that spell was aimed down at the river, directly at Crud.

37

DIRTBAG

The water around Crud began to roil, forming a peaked whitecapped circle with Crud at its center.

"Good day! The Minister will be here in just a few minutes." The Magician spoke in a booming singsong way, as though he were giving the morning announcement over the loudspeaker. "Kindly wait for her to arrive."

Crud's Holy Terror squirmed out of Bethesda's arms and flapped his sodden wings, his eyes on Crud, but the Magician warned, "Stay where you are or I will drown the boy before you get near him."

Down below, Crud was struggling to stay afloat as the whirlpool spun faster. I looked back to see Annika far behind us, while Vanessa's Holy Terror was nowhere in sight. He was probably in Hoboken by now.

The Magicians were getting closer. There were so many of them, they looked like a storm cloud drifting over the river.

Holding on to Bethesda's neck with one hand, I reached into my pocket with my other and felt for my chopsticks. This Magician was not a psycho hipster with tentacles. He wasn't a giant snake. In fact, he looked like a regular person, the sort of guy you might see buying Altoids at the bodega.

Except that he wasn't. And River was out here somewhere, desperate and angry and scared.

"You don't have to do it, Nell," Tom said, watching my hand in my pocket.

"Hang on to me," I told him. I sat up and Tom quickly wrapped his arm around my waist. I took a breath and lifted my chopsticks.

The Magician must have felt the Oomphalos move toward my hands because his head whipped around as I worked the spell.

"I spy the Miten-Ei," he said even as I was still moving my chopsticks. "I noticed that spell in your handbook. Curious. But then your handbook was full of surprises."

How did he know what was in my handbook? I shook off the thought. He was trying to distract me, to pull my focus off him so that the spell wouldn't work.

I concentrated again, put my attention squarely on him as my hands moved through the spell until it was done.

Nothing happened.

"While the Miten-Ei is a handy little spell for certain creatures," the Magician said, "it's totally useless otherwise. Still, it was very wicked of you to even try that one on me." His hands danced in the air and poor Crud was whipped around even more furiously.

Out of the corner of my eye, I caught a blaze of bronze accompanied by the sound of Annika shouting commands as her Holy Terror slammed into the Magician, sending him in a downward topple-spin toward the river. The Magician yelped and his arms flailed but he managed to right himself.

"I was trying to be a nice guy," the Magician bellowed as soon as he had collected himself. His face was flushed with anger, right up to his bald head. "But you ruined it!"

The whirlpool widened as the Magician strengthened his spell, and now the water whipped around with such a fury that Crud was sucked down instantly like a spider being vacuumed off the ceiling.

No, no, no!

Frantically, I sorted through my mind, trying to think of a spell that could help.

There's almost always a way out of a tight spot. Think, think.

Then I remembered something. Reaching into my jacket pocket, I pulled out the three vials. I looked at the Fates behind the glass and chose the one I needed.

"Bethesda, get me close to that Magician," I cried.

"Hang on!"

Tom and I grabbed her neck as she swooped down. The Magician's bald head was below us, his arms outstretched, his hands busy working the spell. I took a breath, unstoppered the vial, and leaned across Bethesda's body, swiftly dropping the Creeping Yeuk onto the Magician's head.

The Creeping Yeuk might have looked like a toilet

bowl cleaner for a dollhouse's bathroom, but that thing was no joke. The Magician instantly began to scratch at himself furiously. He stretched his arms over his shoulders to reach an itch that seemed to elude him. While his hands were busy scratching, they weren't working his spell. The whirlpool was already slowing down. I held my breath as I watched the water settle, searching for a sign of Crud.

"There!" Tom cried.

And yes! Crud's head had reemerged above the waves. His Holy Terror nose-dived toward the river and scooped him out, draping Crud over his shoulder and flying back up to us.

"Well, look who's here, it's Mr. Fishbone!" Vanessa had reappeared with her Holy Terror, who was now hovering in front of the Magician. The man had twisted himself around, one hand reaching up the base of his back and the other one flung over his shoulder and reaching down as he tried to scratch the unreachable itch.

"Mr. Fishbone?" I said. "That name's familiar."

"Meet AOA's new director," Vanessa said, flourishing a hand toward the man with a look of distaste on her face.

Now I remembered. Terrance had told us about him.

"You mean he's an angel?" I asked.

"In name only. Turns out he has been working with the Magicians behind the scenes." She turned to me. "Itching Spell?" she asked.

"Creeping Yeuk."

"Nice." She nodded approvingly. She turned to Mr. Fishbone. "Well, if you're going to act like a dirtbag, Fishbone, you'd better be prepared for some fleas."

The sky darkened, and when I turned I saw the swarm of Magicians only yards away. Heading them up was a short, stout little girl wearing round glasses and a blue tulle dress with a pair of Halloween fairy wings attached to the back. The Minister. My stomach plummeted with dread. She waved at me, her fingers wiggling.

"Everyone, go, go, go!" Vanessa said. "Dead ahead! Aim for the left ear!"

38

THE OLD MAN IN THE HOSPITAL GOWN

I f there had been any question about where we were headed, there were no doubts now. Up ahead, sprouting out of a small island in the middle of the river, was an old man in a hospital gown. The Statue of Liberty. I could see the statue's cranky face, his hair standing up in clumps, and I wondered if the child who'd casted it had only ever seen the real statue at a distance, where I guessed it could be mistaken for an old man in a hospital gown.

Vanessa was ahead of us as we flew toward the statue. Just when it looked like she was going to ram right into it, her Holy Terror soared upward at a sharp angle until he reached the statue's head.

"Hold on tight back there!" Bethesda warned. Tom flopped down on his belly next to me and put his arms over mine and around Bethesda's neck a second before she too swooped up. We were vertical now, with nothing between our feet and the river but sky. I squeezed my eyes shut as we went up, up, up.

When we stopped, I opened my eyes. We were right

next to the Statue of Liberty's face. I could have reached out and touched his nostrils.

"You'll have to go through the ear!" Vanessa cried to us, pointing to a hole in the middle of the statue's ear, as her Holy Terror flittered in place in the air.

Bethesda maneuvered around so that she was horizontal again beside the statue's face, though there was still a gap between her back and the statue's ear.

"It's as close as I can get, babies," Bethesda called to us.

"We'll have to jump," I said to Tom. I could barely get the words out of my mouth.

"I know." He held my hand and we both got to our feet. I looked down at the empty space between us and the ear.

"We're jumping toward River," I said.

He squeezed my hand. "Ready? One, two, three . . ."

We both leapt. I felt my feet hit metal with a *clang!* and I immediately slipped, jerking my hand out of Tom's, and I slid through the statue's ear canal, landing in a large dark chamber on my butt.

"Ah, Ms. Batista, graceful as always."

The room was so dark that it took me a minute to see him, but I knew the voice well.

Mr. Boot stuck out a hand and helped me to my feet, just as Tom entered the chamber as well.

Standing beside Mr. Boot was a woman with fine white hair and a face that looked like it had seen far too much.

Mary Carpenter.

"Where is he?" I asked her, but before she could answer

I saw him. He was slumped down in a dark recess of the chamber, utterly still.

"River!" I rushed over and knelt down beside him. He looked awful. His skin had a feverish sheen and his eyes were bleary with exhaustion.

"You shouldn't be here, Nell," River murmured. "You have to go home. The Wickets . . ."

"I know. You're closing them. And it looks like it's killing you."

"I've got a Bloznik Ward locked and loaded," Vanessa said the moment she entered the chamber, followed by Crud.

"Where's Annika?" Crud asked.

"Knock, knock!" a voice called out.

Standing at the chamber's opening was a chubby little girl in glasses, holding a wand with a glittery star on the tip. She adjusted her fairy wings, which had gone askew, then did a quick two-step so that her tap shoes clanked against the metal floor as she stepped. She grimaced at the sound, then giggled. "Sorry. Just had to try that. Anyway, let me count." She pointed her wand at us one by one. "Now that's one, two, three—" She stopped when she saw Mary. Her doughy face twitched with displeasure. "Mary Carpenter. It's been a long time. You're a slippery little thing. Sneaking around the Nigh like a rat. Causing trouble. You've aged."

"I've lived," Mary said evenly.

The Minister didn't like that reply. She pushed her lips out, which, had she been an actual child, would have been a pout, but on the Minister seemed like the expression of a discontented old lady. "Yes, we'll have to do something about that. Oh, and look, we have our darling River down there on the floor." The Minister's voice turned treacly. "And there's what's-her-name." She waved her wand dismissively at Vanessa. "And hello, Mr. Boot, you stupid, stupid man. Regretting your decision yet?"

"Not at all, Minister," Mr. Boot replied impassively.

"What decision?" I asked.

"Oh, you don't know?" The Minister squealed with delight. "Mr. Boot used to work for me. He trained the little Human children to cast. Very good at his job too."

I turned to Mr. Boot. "Is that true?"

He looked at me and for once, he appeared at a loss for words.

"It is true, Nell," Tom broke in.

"You knew?" I said to Tom, shocked. "Why didn't you tell me?"

"Because he's not who he used to be." He glanced at Mr. Boot, with whom he'd always had a prickly relationship. "Neither one of us are."

Mr. Boot nodded at Tom, and I thought I detected a look of gratitude in his expression.

"If you understand your enemy, which Mr. Boot most certainly does," Mary added, "you'll never be defeated."

"Well said, well said!" The Minister clapped her little hands, then looked around the chamber with mock concern. "Oopsie, I think one of you is missing! Hmm. Maybe she's still out there?" She pointed at the ear canal, through which we could see the sky outside.

And there was Annika, held in the arms of her Holy Terror, whose wings were flapping as he hovered in place. Surrounding them was a fortress of Magicians, layers deep on all sides. I'm sure Annika was terrified, but you would never have known it. She had willed her beautiful face to be a picture of cool indifference, as though she were simply sitting in math class, bored out of her mind and waiting for the period bell to ring. In that moment, I took back every unkind thought I had ever had about her. Whatever else she was—the good, the bad, and the annoying—she was also one of the bravest people I knew.

39

THE MISSING SPELL

"You'd be astonished at how much certain Folk will pay for a pair of bronze angel wings," the Minister said. "Easy to slice off with the right spell. And then *weeee*, down they go, into the Hudson." She flapped her hands as though she were splashing in water.

"Don't!" River had struggled to his feet and now was heading toward the ear canal. "Let her go, and you can have me."

Mr. Boot stopped him with a hand on his shoulder. "I'm sure the Minister would be delighted to have her most gifted caster returned to her. But that won't be enough. She's after something more now."

The Minister's eyes narrowed at this, but she said nothing.

"Something interesting happened on the Brooklyn Bridge all those years ago," Mr. Boot continued.

"Obviously," the Minister snapped. "Silly little girl did a spell. *Poof!* Made the entire bridge collapse. Old story. Are you just finding out about it now, Mr. Tardy-To-The-Party?"

"That's not what the spell did, and you know it."

The Minister was silent. She rolled her shoulders, making her fake fairy wings shiver.

"What did the spell do?" Crud asked.

"It released me from her," Mary said, nodding toward the Minister. "I felt it right away, even as I was tumbling off the bridge. I knew it. I knew I was free from her."

"It was just the accident that did it," the Minister said dismissively. "Just the shock of it."

"I wasn't shocked about the accident," Mary said. "Why would I be? I made the bridge collapse. I casted it to fall, with all of you on it. I was desperate, like River, and I didn't see any other way out except destruction. But then something happened. There was a little girl on the banks of the river who was creating a spell. She didn't even know she was doing it. You know better than anyone, Minister, that spells are very old things. Secret things. Passed down by the authority of magic itself. But every so often, a new spell is created, when desire meets need at the exact right time. That little girl must have felt very sorry for me. That's all, but it was enough, and her spell released me, and you knew it. I didn't understand what had happened. I've been trying for years to make sense of it all. Why was I able to go back home when the other children couldn't? Over the years, I tracked down everyone I could who had been at the bridge that day, looking for answers. And recently, I found out about a certain Fennick."

"That's why they took the magic from Tilda," said Crud. "To remove that spell from her?"

"Magic, particularly powerful magic like this, can behave much like a virus, Mr. Butterbank," Mr. Boot said. "It will do what it needs to in order to survive. That spell slipped out of the Minister's grasp, and it waited for the right Magician to come along. It lay dormant for years, waiting for the Magician who was supposed to have it." Mr. Boot nodded toward me.

"Me? Wait, me?" I cried. "But I don't have the spell! I hardly have any spells at all, and a lot of them are pretty much trash."

"You have a spell in your handbook that has no name, which means it's a new spell. And that's rare. Unfortunately, when the AOA examined your handbooks, Fishbone saw the spell too. He grew suspicious. He was the one who fast-forwarded your Initiation Trials, and he was the one who wanted to make sure you failed yours, Nell. It would remove you from my protection, and the protection of the AOA. It would leave you exposed so that you could be grabbed and taken to the Nigh and the spell could be removed."

"But I tried the spell. It doesn't work," I said.

"Exactly. You see it's useless." The Minister turned to me, her eyes fixed on mine as if no one else was in the room. "It doesn't take long. You wouldn't feel a thing. We'd simply be removing what you don't need anyway. You'll have the tiniest little scar, hardly noticeable." She touched the side of her neck. "I can do it right now, and then guess what? Everyone goes home. Yay! Happy ending. The other option is I can simply let the girl out there fall into the river."

"If the spell is useless," I countered, "why do you want it so badly?"

"Ms. Batista, you finally are using that famous brain of yours," said Mr. Boot.

An idea started to form. "If spells can be created," I asked Mr. Boot, "can they also be destroyed?"

"Not easily, but yes. The more times a spell has been used, the harder it is to destroy it. But a new spell is vulnerable."

"You know what?" the Minister said, her voice cracking with anger. "I think I'll just go out there and tell the Magicians to cut off those wings now. Toodles." She walked out of the statue and leapt into the air, where she lifted her wand.

I turned to Mr. Boot. "She'll do it!"

"Magic isn't simply about directions in a handbook," Mr. Boot said. "I've been trying to teach that to you bloody plonkers since the Last Chance Club first started. Almost anyone can learn to do most spells. But this is a powerful spell. It requires a powerful magician to perform it."

"Which I'm not."

"Great magic works at the intersection where desire meets desperate need. You're there right now, Ms. Batista."

I took a breath and began to work the spell with no

name. As my hands moved, I thought about Dad's face. I could see his eyes widen at the sight of River coming through the front door. I could see the disbelief, then the tears. I could feel my father's happiness exploding in my own chest. I could *feel* the spell now. I could feel the tingling strength of it building around my hands, expanding, like it was a living thing that was feeding on my thoughts, getting stronger and stronger. I could see River walking into our bedroom again, putting his hand on the top bunk, touching the quilt that he hadn't slept under for three years. And me, going to sleep knowing that River was there, and would be there when I woke up in the morning, and every morning after. My eyes were so full of tears now that I couldn't see what my hands were doing, but it didn't matter. I closed my eyes. I thought about all those other stolen children walking through their own front doors, the shock on their parents' faces, the unbelievable joy that filled their bodies. Somewhere I heard a scream and then more screams, but I kept going, I couldn't stop. It was as if my hands had become the Oomphalos and they were moving with the rhythm of an ancient current that had passed though the hands of magicians for thousands of years, and I was a part of that current now. I worked the spell until the tingling in my hands subsided, then stopped, and I felt the spell leave my body all at once, like a breath that had been held far too long.

"Sheesh, remind me never to make you mad again. You are a beast."

I opened my eyes and there was Annika in front of me. I threw my arms around her, and started sobbing all over again. We are both pull-away people, but neither one of us pulled away until Annika said, "Are you getting mucus in my hair?"

"Yes."

"Okay. This is over."

Mary was standing beside Annika, her arm looped through River's. He was weak but on his feet, and now he smiled at me, that new and strange lopsided smile with the scar on his upper lip that hadn't been there before he'd been taken.

"You did it," Mary said to me. "It's over."

"Over, over?" I looked at River.

"Over, over," he replied. "I can feel it, like Mary said."

Mr. Boot approached with his hand extended and a rare smile on his face. "Well done, Ms. Batista."

"Really, Luther?" Vanessa gave Mr. Boot a little shove with her hip. "Well done and a handshake? After what this girl just did!" She hugged me to her. "That was some sick magic."

"What happened to the Magicians?" I asked, looking outside at the sky, now empty.

"They fell straight into the river like raindrops," Vanessa said, "All of them, including the Minister. Splat, right into the water. It was a pretty high drop. I'd be surprised if any of them managed to survive."

"The spell did that?"

"All these years," Mary said, "the Magicians have been taking pieces from the children they trained to cast—pieces of their lives, pieces of their energy. They fueled their own magic with it, you know. Your spell stripped them of it in one fell swoop. Which means you not only released River, you released the other children too."

"But how will they—?"

"We'll find the other kids, don't worry," Vanessa said. "We'll take them back home again." She stuck her fingers in her mouth and let out a shrill whistle. "There! The Anywhere Taxi should be downstairs in a minute. Now let's get you guys out of here."

"But I failed the Initiation Trial," I said. "Won't the AOA perform the Umglick Spell on me?"

"After what you guys did here? Ha! I wouldn't be surprised if the AOA gives you all VIP swag bags."

"What do you mean?"

"Well, mostly the AOA swag bags are pretty lame. You get them at the AOA conferences, and they have stuff like little bottles of shampoo and keyrings and miniature chocolate bars. But in the VIP swag bags, they also give you a free wish. The AOA don't like to give out wishes—messes with the order of things—but every so often, they'll make an exception. I have a feeling you've got a VIP swag bag coming your way, so start thinking of a wish, pal!"

My biggest wish had already come true. River was coming home. But here's the funny thing about wishes: you never actually run out of them.

40

ᕫWISHES

"Crackers. Now we're talking, kids!"
Ruth raised her fist and smashed the packets of saltines that came with tomato soup in Crud's school lunch. She opened the packets and poured the crumbs in her hands. Recently, a dishwasher at her father's restaurant had taught her how to tell fortunes by reading leftover food. Since she'd been bringing Crud lunch from the restaurant every day, she'd been perfecting her fortune-telling skills by using Crud's nasty school lunches.

"You first today, Gorgeous George." Ruth handed the crumbs to Tom. Tom side-eyed me and smiled, then closed his eyes. He shook the crumbs in his closed fist and spilled them out on the lunch table.

"Okay, let's see . . ." Ruth stood up and studied the crumbs. "Hmm, that's interesting. You have what looks like an iceberg, which means romance is looming."

"Romance is always looming in Tom's readings," Crud said.

"Can I help it if this is a very romantic lunch table?" Ruth replied.

Across the lunchroom, I saw Jordan sitting with his Boo Crew, their table strewn with a collection of DIY ghost gizmos. The Boo Crew seemed to have doubled its membership in the past few weeks, no doubt due to Jordan's sudden celebrity. His Spook-O-Meter had led him to a sale bin in Skull 'n Bones, where he found an old mason jar with a tag on it saying that the jar contained the ghost of Blackbeard the pirate. Since then, Jordan had been carrying the jar around in his backpack, charging kids two bucks each to see it. So maybe a Code 10-81 meant preventing someone from becoming a pint-sized swindler.

"Okay, River, you're next," Ruth said, and she poured saltine crumbs in his hand.

It had taken a solid three weeks for people at school to stop staring at River as though he were a specimen floating in a jar of formaldehyde. By now everyone knew his story. Or anyway, they knew the story we'd told them: That after he'd been missing for three years, I had found River sitting on a bench in Washington Square Park. That he didn't remember much about his time away. That it might come back to him someday, but for now, he was trying to return to the life he had before everything happened. This was pretty much what he had told Dad as well. Neither one of us wanted to lie to Dad, but there were rules about the Nigh, as Mr. Boot had told us in the Anywhere Taxi, and one of those rules was that we could never tell others about it. Dad was so beside himself to have River back that, for now anyway, he accepted the explanation.

River shook the crumbs in his hands, then tossed them on the table. Ruth scrutinized them, her fingers tapping at her lower lip. "It looks like a muffin. Hmm. What's a muffin mean?"

"Are you asking me?" River said.

"Maybe. Does a muffin mean anything to you?" Ruth asked in a spooky voice.

Annika rolled her eyes. "Is this actually what you guys do at this table?"

"Yeah. What do they do at the Goddess Table?" Crud asked.

"Mostly they talk trash about you people."

"Admit it." I nudged her with my elbow. "You're glad you switched tables."

"Well." Her eyes flitted across the table to River. "Most days."

Ruth gathered up the crumbs again. "Now you, genius," she said to me.

I held out my hands and she poured the crumbs into them. I closed my eyes and shook the crumbs in my fist, then threw them on the table.

Ruth stared at them for a solid minute before she pointed at a pile of crumbs off by themselves. "That there looks like a key."

"What does that mean?" I asked.

"It means there are going to be big changes in your life."

Well, that was definitely accurate. Since we'd come back from the Nigh, a lot had changed and I was still getting used to it. Sometimes I'd wake up in the morning and gasp when I saw a pair of feet hanging off the top bunk until I remembered River was home, *actually home*. Dad and I still stole glances at River while we ate dinner or watched TV. I think we both half expected him to vanish again at any moment.

River had changed too. That thin scar on his mouth, which lifted his upper lip slightly, giving him a permanent sneer, was a constant reminder that he'd returned to us a different person. He was quieter now, and more distant. There were times I'd be talking to him and his attention would suddenly drift elsewhere—maybe back to the Nigh. He had terrible nightmares that would make him cry out in his sleep. When that happened, I would jump out of bed and watch helplessly as he tossed in his top bunk, his face damp with sweat, before slipping off to sleep again.

One of the biggest changes was he stopped telling stories. Maybe it was simply that, at thirteen, he was done with storytelling. But I think there was more to it. I think that, after his time in the Nigh, he was frightened of his own imagination. So now I told him stories. Each night, as we were lying in bed, I told him about things the chess hustlers in the park had done and how the woman across the street kept an actual goat in her apartment for a while, and how my lab partner Gretchen Mousekey skewered her ear with a toothpick. They were true stories, the stories of all the things he'd missed while he was in the Nigh. He listened to them in silence. He was often so quiet that I sometimes thought he'd fallen asleep, but when I stopped talking he'd say, "Tell me more."

Dad found River a therapist and the school was helping to bring him up to speed in his classes, but I think it was Annika who made the biggest difference for him. She showed up at our apartment one day with a pack of cards and taught him how to play a game called Spit. It was a lightning-fast game. You had to pay complete attention the whole time. At first Annika won every game. That girl wouldn't throw a game if her life depended on it. After a while River got better at Spit. He was able to focus for longer. His reflexes grew faster. They played game after game for hours, laughing and calling out "Spit!", the winner throwing up their arms, fists clenched. The petty part of me wondered if Annika had chosen Spit because only two people could play it. Maybe she had, who knows, but anyway, she was helping River, and that was all that mattered.

There was another change too. The AOA had given everyone in the Last Chance Club a swag bag to reward us for our efforts. Vanessa had been right. They were

VIP swag bags. We each got a pair of sunglasses, a T-shirt that said I'm a l'il angel with a picture of a racoon with a halo over its head, some miniature shampoo bottles, tiny chocolate bars, and a travel neck pillow with AOA embroidered on it. And each one of us also got a wish.

Annika wished to go to a track and field training camp over Christmas vacation—in Paris. Crud said he'd made his wish but he wouldn't tell us what it was. Tom wasn't given a swag bag since he wasn't officially a member of the Last Chance Club, but that was okay, because I made my wish for him. I had to talk to Tom about it first, of course, and then Mr. Boot, who needed a little convincing, but in the end he agreed.

My wish was that Tom could stay in the Hither and live with Mr. Boot. Vanessa made arrangements for the Anywhere Taxi to take Tom to Mrs. Nerriberry's whenever he liked so he could visit his ghosts, as well as Lysander, who had settled in very nicely to life in Piddlebank.

I went back with Tom once to visit Mrs. Nerriberry. I said it was because I wanted to see the Nigh again after so much had changed there, but it was mostly because I missed her. Over a platter of Iced Nippers, she told us that many Folk had left the City to go to quieter places and live more in the old Folk ways again. Piddlebank was getting a little too crowded, in her opinion, and she was busier than ever with creatures who were getting accidentally stepped on by ex-City people who didn't know any better. The Magicians, the few that were left, had fled to far-flung places, and she hoped that was the end of them, although every so often there would be a rumor that the Minister was sighted. But that was probably Folks' imagination, she said. Reynold had told her that several new Wickets had opened, although she never saw the point of them anyway, when living in one world kept you busy enough. Oh, and Solly had been true to her word and brought Mary Carpenter to visit. "You could speak to her just like she was a regular person," gushed Mrs. Nerriberry. "She fed my little cattywumpus a sardine out of her very own hand and she said I had one of the finest little creature hospitals this side of the Nigh. I tell you, it was the proudest day of my life!"

"Oh hey, kids," Ruth said as she collected the cracker crumbs in her hand, "there's a new horror flick at the Barton this weekend. It's about this archeologist who digs up a monster that's covered in fungus. I've seen this movie seven times, and it never gets old. Who's in?"

"Pass," I said.

"Pass," said River.

"Passing too," said Tom.

"You couldn't pay me enough," said Annika.

Ruth shook her head in disappointment. "You guys are such a bunch of chickens. What about you, Crud?"

"I'm in."

"Yes! Saturday at seven o'clock. It's a date," Ruth said.

Crud smiled to himself, a small, secret smile. Under the table, Tom grabbed my hand and squeezed it, his eyes flitting over to Crud. I nodded, understanding.

Now we'd all gotten our wishes.

Acknowledgments

Years ago, I was lucky enough to attend a Kurt Vonnegut lecture, during which he advised us all to "get a gang." He was right. We all need a gang; we need those special people who root for us when we feel discouraged and tap us on the shoulder when we are about to take a wrong turn.

As a writer, I am blessed with an exceptional gang.

Thanks to my husband, Adam, and my son, Ian, who patiently listened as I sorted through all the possible spells Nell and her friends might use to disable a giant snake.

Thanks to my brilliant agent, Alice Tasman, who has been my rock all these years. What would I do without you? I am so grateful to Jennifer Weltz and the entire team at Jean V. Naggar Literary Agency, my extended family.

Huge thanks to my editor and manuscript magician, Karen Wojtyla, whose insight and discernment were so crucial to shaping this series.

Thanks to Jen Bricking for her mind-blowingly gorgeous cover art.

Lastly, thanks to Nicole Fiorica, Nicole Valdez, Thad Whittier, and the entire team at Margaret K. McElderry Books, who did all the difficult behind-the-scenes work to send this book out into the world.

When Sylvie realizes her LARPing summer camp is actually full of real monsters, she'll need to put on the performance of a lifetime!

"Henning's clever premise allows her to explore a panorama of monsters, and her brisk, lively style deftly balances both frights and humor.... A mirthful monster mashup."

–*Kirkus Reviews*

A sweetly spooky story perfect for fans of *Ghost Squad* and *Hotel Transylvania*!

PRINT AND EBOOK EDITIONS AVAILABLE
Margaret K. McElderry Books   simonandschuster.com/kids

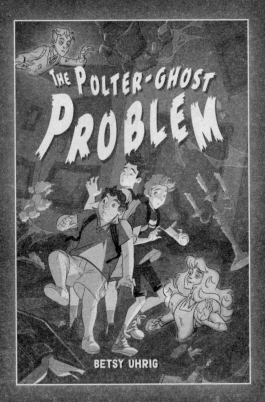

Stranger Things meets ***Sideways Stories from Wayside School*** in this zany supernatural adventure about a reluctant boy medium who must track down an enchanted book to defeat an unearthly nemesis.

"Spectral silliness with high appeal."
—*Kirkus Reviews*

FIELD GUIDE
TO THE
SUPERNATURAL
UNIVERSE

#1 *New York Times* Bestselling Author
ALYSON NOËL

What magic lives in the ivy-covered house?

An enchanting family story from award-winning author Hilary McKay

"Utterly enchanting . . . an instant classic."
—*New York Times Book Review*

★ "A perfect mix of magic and realism."
—*School Library Journal*, starred review

★ "A captivating world to fall into."
—*Horn Book*, starred review

★ "McKay draws on her genius in creating amiable, chaotic families containing members with their own personal dramas."
—*BCCB*, starred review

PRINT AND EBOOK EDITIONS AVAILABLE
Margaret K. McElderry Books • simonandschuster.com/kids